Trapped in the Cracks

Clarence R. Williams

TCC Books

ISBN:
978-0615613888 (original pbk. © 2012)
978-0692454381 (revised, © 2015; finalized, © 2018)

Cover design by Clarence Williams

TrappedInTheCracks.com

Manufactured in the United States of America

Thank you for reading this book. I hope you enjoy its tales, prose and poetry. If so, please recommend *Trapped in the Cracks* to your friends by posting the website (TrappedintheCracks.com) on your blog or social media page and/or leaving a review on Amazon (tinyurl.com/TrappedAuthor) or Goodreads (good-reads.com/ClarenceWms). The author, who is working with a shoestring staff and budget, greatly appreciates your invaluable time, support, and constructive criticism. Thank you.
#TrappedInTheCracks

Dedicated to the women
who, since my birth, have
suffered through this
journey with me; my
mother, Treva, and my
sisters, Chyna and Charisma.
I have *always* wanted
more for you.
Through all hardship, you
have been my motivation
to endure.
More than life itself,
I love you.

Defend the
poor and fatherless: do justice to the afflicted and
needy.
Deliver the
poor and needy: rid them of
the hand of the wicked.

Psalms 82:3-4

Trapped in the Cracks

Stages of frustration blanket the battle of haste and patience when conquering contagious complacence.

Constant Struggle

Sunshine is sliced by white blinds. Its bright lines span pine, pots and pans. Beneath a ceiling fan sits a sinking man—deep in thought, reeling in his feelings. Concealing those feelings with reasoning. As his seedlings are sleeping, he's eating and thinking of a plan to plant them in grand, expectant land.

Though negligent, at present, his Mrs. is embittering him, his kids are missing him, and his gig is killing him—all week, six to six, with a chisel, chipping a seemingly endless pit of bricks. Admittedly, he emitted a pessimistic disposition.

Sick of feeling like the dispirited who built pyramids, he was at a period of focusing on myriad miscreants and old foes—potential targets for rolls of dough. Sitting in the kitchen licking fingers from jerk chicken and reminiscing, his wish at the minute was to hit a lick for a meal ticket. But before he attempts to fulfill his wishes, he'll clean a sink full of sticky dishes for his Mrs.

As a little kid, Nick did the work he preferred, but didn't go along with the herd of so-called cool kids who blurted curse words in school and weren't concerned with who heard. He was an introvert and a bit of a nerd but had heart from the start. So he rarely cared for the affairs of others but would go berserk if he observed an undeserving learner disturbed by bullies in hoodies who often played hooky. This was when Nick was known for well-woven poems, being on the honor roll, and proposing ocean strolls on the coast with old folks. He's now known for routine schemes for sneaky thieves who've sold stolen rings and bling, hoodwinked kings and knights of grime, pulled off heists of Brinks that he designed, and scoffed at evil deeds and crime. As well as his past hustles, cash bundles, and drug smuggles, that bought costly cufflinks, minks, and fine wine.

The transformation came in his mid-teens, with the burden to urgently get, for his kin, more green—money for rent, consistently decent meals, and utility bills. As the phase made his ways change, his grades strained to remain on page and he failed to graduate.

For him, and his sister, it was tough coming up. It wasn't as rough as life in a mud hut—the kind you find in slums nigh the dump of a country trying but bungling their rise—but they barely had enough. As a pupil, Nick never knew what it meant to get new boots or suits for school. At the very best, he could pray to play in shoes from Payless. Being that poor could make you lay in bed for days, staying depressed and wasting away. Trying to live life deprived was like fighting a dreadful battle uphill from the flying belt of a treadmill: Futile moves to make noodles and frugal bread into a real meal.

With meager means to succeed and so many ways to fail, it was difficult to deal with the appeal of chrome-wheeled automobiles and not be tempted to steal. This is the needy's Achilles' heel.

Where Nick was raised, to make a rent payment, poor people pry pennies from the pavement. And when people in poverty can't meet their needs, they seek to profit from the lottery, or possibly a robbery by stealing property. Some swallow their pride to borrow a dollar just to drown their sorrows at the bottom of a brown bottle. In many poor communities, the ideal opportunity was to learn skills to earn a salary in a factory or steel mill.

Like many men, Nick Bernard's heart was hardened in this garden of darkness—provinces of little promise—where the harvest is rarely pardoned, or harnessed as bronze starlets or artists of prominence. But topless harlots are often made of the jobless and harmless, and carcasses in carpets have been found behind markets. It was given for rent, but untilled and untended. Also known as the jungle, or forest, it had few florists.

But promptings of caution often blossomed. Starting in kindergarten, or the boulevard, common doctrines, options and margins are carved without markings. This unfarmed plot, formed by columns of blocks, is where rotting crops are often shot, sometimes for not minding advice, or those unwritten guiding signs, that might've enlightened their lives—the downtrodden and forgotten who dream of reaching stardom from Sodom. But the only heroes most know are those that sold coke by the boatload then doled out coats to the broke when it got cold.

This was home, where so-called Negros and Latinos, and the occasional gringo, speak street lingo with amigos shooting free throws or rolling cee-low through weed smoke, or that of cigarillos, for a few c-notes, while being bit by mosquitoes as big as flamingos.

After a couple months of busting his butt in construction, Nick decided his cash production would be better back in corruption. He could still vividly envision the repercussions of his latest conviction. But the addiction, and seduction, of the syndicate, in addition to his compulsive ambition, cinched his decision.

Being a player in the cocaine game was the hastiest way he knew to make paper. The thought alone changed him into a salivating alligator. But being an easily attainable drug trader would place him back inside a box the size and shape of an elevator for the remainder of his days. Life as a day laborer was safer, but the low wage he made came as slow as a glacier, so lately his only prayer has been to pull a major caper. He felt like a failure and didn't want to ask a friend or neighbor for a favor. He would rather brave danger like a crusader or gladiator.

Higher primates gyrate their waists late on Fridays at raves as a way to celebrate, chase mates, or medicate.

Club Love

It was imminent, within days Nick would implement an intricate hit he had blueprinted with redundant repetition—consistent with his reputation for precision. It was a risk that could get him killed. However, he felt it was a risk worth giving his kids somewhere more fitting to live.

In the coming days, the cunning assailant may raise to see the Sun's emanating rays as a sign of dangers to come and the grating pain that awaits, rather than just a giant flame to warm his face from outer space, for shit is about to hit the blades in spates, all for the sake of getting paid. Therefore, what may be his last day of grace, he chose to celebrate—get faded and wasted till he was dazed in a faint haze that would erase all trepidation. He thought a safe place to get drunk, and entertained, was a club's crazy maze of intoxicating dames oscillating to the bass.

Nick called a group of dudes he knew from previous criminal maneuvers. Ex-shooters who used to scam banks, scale bales of weight—cocaine and copious opiates—with odious associates, and handle shanks like fangs of snakes. It was already late when he made the call, so only four of eight were able to make the haul.

They pulled up in his cousin's custom truck in front of Club Love. Spring, autumn or summer, this club was jumping. It wasn't in the slums, so anyone in the city over twenty would come. The atmosphere reeked with a cyclone of both steep and cheap cologne. Beats had a grown tone of trombones, saxophones, trumpets pumping and drums thumping. Both slim and thick chicks were in rhythm and bumping. Most who showed up just wanted to toast cups, get a buzz and have some fun. Rough thugs would never attempt to cut a rug, but they would summon a woman with an awesome bosom or rump to brush up on or hug. A few of the buffoons were loose and acting a fool from too many cups of juice with gin or Grey Goose.

Occasionally, girls in Dior prance past the door, clap their hands, chant and roar. With only a glance at lapels and pants, they can report as to who wore a band and which man wore which brands. As if they were monetary matadors, those with plans for more are placed in a trance to scan and explore the expanse of the dance floor to catch a trace of a man's finances before building a rapport. Then they coolly move towards men who look like they can afford Michael Kors, a new Accord, and a mortgage, of which the audience had an obvious short-age.

Of course, some men, willing to spend money for inter-course, pretend to be rich to enhance their chances of getting handpicked simple chicks—some would call them idiots—to sit in their whips. Those equally simple men—some would call them tricks—take a stance and make an advance to implore girls who would normally ignore their demands of romance if they were knowingly poor. It was noted that some were whores, but they too were adored.

Within and all around, your typical visitors were visible, though not all were admissible: Like most evenings, many cheaply-geared, weird guys disappear to the rear with a beer near their peers—a court of cowering flowers convened to lean on the wall as not to fall. As patrons paraded, passed glasses and paid, the barmaid raked green in fast like blades of grass. And unsuspecting marks learn a hard lesson using credit or debit at the bar, when they discover extra charges on their cards. On this day, to their dismay, the games of underage girls didn't persuade the big rock-shaped blockades under surveil-lance to risk a raid by breaking regulations that forbade their fortes of masquerading, misbehaving, and risqué forays.

For four hours in this loud crowd, Nick and his pals drowned in an unaccountable amount of brown brandy, Crown Royal and cola. As the night drew to an end, Nick got sick and had to risk losing his crew to use the restroom to spew brews through tissues over the stool. Known by many in barbarous conglomerates to be a once prosperous rhinoceros, he cautiously hid his moderate liquor tolerance. Coming from the restroom, he bumped into a cutie with a strong strut, long judged as a slut, who used to hump a chump he once snuffed in the gut with an uppercut in his school lunchroom.

Nick was no punk; he had moxie—cocky as if he embodied Rocky and played hockey for hobby. He didn't strike like he applied the karate of Miyagi, but he had a one-two as mighty as Mike and Scottie. He was always up to thump—stand, take and land a punch like a man—but he wasn't dumb; he stepped and slept with a gun tucked.

He recalled the small-waisted chick from his last days in the hallways waiting to take school pics. Since skipping with truant students, she grew from a toothpick to too thick. Due to her well-known keen eye for wealthy, clean guys, she was seen as a gold-digging hawk. After a second to gawk, Nick made small talk before he continued his walk.

"Yo, what's up with you, girl?" asked Nick, as he tapped her arm to change her focus. It was clear he wasn't noticed.

"Shit. Chillin'. What you tryin' to get into?" replied his former schoolmate, assuming he was another potential date.

Nick gave her a strange look. "Naw, not me. I'm good," he said, turning down her apparent offer to trade bed covers for his coffers. "I remember you from school, that's all."

"Oh, yeah? You went to Juneau, too?" asked the cutie.

"I did. I was in the eleventh when you were in the tenth. I see you've grown up since then. And out," said Nick, followed by a slight grin of admiration for her physical graduation. She was definitely the type to spark his imagination.

"Well, I'll take that as a compliment," she said.

Nick nodded. "Definitely."

On her opposite arm, another man gained the confidence to prove his dominance and charm. Without giving comment, Nick let the incompetent prick feel as though he had made a big accomplishment.

"I recon he's beckoning for questioning," said Nick, gesturing in the fella's direction.

"It happens," she said, then blushed and shrugged.

"So, it was nice seeing you," said Nick, backing away. "Take care."

"If I don't, who will?" she sassed with puckered lips—used to hurt men whom she assumed to be suckers and wimps—then presented her latest 6-foot-8-inch victim with unmitigated attention.

Nick smirked at the jerk that wasted no time sliding in to work his corny words and flirts on the snooty acting cutie (maybe due to her once being roofied), then smoothly continued from the restroom where he had puked profusely.

Like uncanny eye-candy, it was quite a sight for pansies to see her fancy panties and genes cling to every seam inside here jeans. She had little inner beauty, but absolutely an unusually voluptuous bootie. And what routinely ensued a view of her boobies was dudes speaking rudely. They were like groupies.

The blue jay in the cage sang to keep from going insane, to cope, and to maintain hope of one day coasting home.

Jane's Change

Trusting a lusting, gutsy guy, the busty girl from the now musty club got drunk and succumbed to a random handsome man's lame game and fables of NBA fame and acclaim. In the vain chick's brain, the image of getting paid lit a flame. Her name was Jane. From so many scrubby and hungry days in the muggy rain, she lost all shame and any remaining disdain of being slain. So lately she gravitated to instant gratification and gain.

In her estimation, cleaning stains and waiting tables was no way to feed a queen's dreams and aspirations. Daily, drinking milkshakes with Bailey's, she held a fantasy free of vultures but full of pictures of her perfect figure on Twitter, in winter wearing short furs, as a big tipper of chauffeurs, at dinner eating rare hors d'oeuvres, and purchasing purses worth as much as a plot of preserved earth. Her envy was greedy, needing everything immediately.

It didn't help that her zesty bestie was a sex-selling arrestee. Raised to be a survivor in Carolina, Delilah was a liar, crier, and admirer of bikers and shysters, who provided pesos for potatoes, designer totes, recliners, fine china, and diapers for Elijah, in exchange of her vagina and saliva. She would've been kinder if she simply worked in a diner.

It had been six weeks since Jane slid, pissed and numb, from under the crushing thumb of a slick pimp. His chauvinist grip was a steel clinched fist the equivalent of Napoleon's. A fish fresh out of Waterloo, she was now seeking a prince who was richer, and hotter too. She lacked the means to leave the track completely, so she weaved between street weeds and cracks discreetly. But shunned scrubs in the club and on the bus who were cursed with the worst luck—not enough bucks, bud or drug sums for her type of fun.

The flirting jerk's cheap chirping in the club convinced the skirt to sit in his Benz, fitted with tints, silver rims and trim. But she didn't know he was pretending, and had misrepresented his expenses. He rented the Benz on weekends to trick chicks into thinking he was willing and able to spend dividends—which he simply invented—on them.

Speeding on Peach Street, from the passenger seat she got a streaking peek of a fiend, seemingly from a repeating dream theme, sitting behind a shopping cart stocked with parts of cars. If police were on patrol with an iPhone they could hold a photo of the solo hobo to show all those defiant minors, with no advisors, who desire to be beguiling liars, reviled fighters and so-called riders. Maybe to inspire a child mired in trials to be kinder, wiser than MacGyver, and aspired to be a firefighter or Freightliner driver.

Knowing, through seeing, that on any given night you can unexpectedly relive some bad deed, or missed opportunity, that you can't outrun, you're repeatedly uneasy when thinking of eventually dreaming—bringing your bleakest minutes in misery creeping back into your memory. As if silently dying, it leaves you terrified, and the certainty of reality unverified.

Likewise, the emaciated face of the fiend made Jane think of the strangest dream, as though she were seeing it occur in scenes, as seen many evenings previously:

"To the unadjusted, the easily detectable smell must be unbearable, detestable. Aligned beside couch sectionals were garbage receptacles filled with rotted cottage, cabbage mixed with other indigestible vegetables, old apples, toads and scalpels, unforgettable swine intestinals, irreparable medical spectacles—

I can see felines crying and trying to find mealtime over obstacles. There was a cool breeze of about thirty-two degrees. Sitting in a puddle amongst rubble in the middle of an alley, sadly, the seat of my trousers are soaked, as well as my flower-patterned blouse and powder-blue coat. I was freezing

*in a three-inch-deep sea. In frigid liquid, my rigid, unkempt
digits were positioned in holes of knitted penny loafers. But I
had no will to live, so I continued to sit still.*

*I wiped my dry mouth, unaware of my whereabouts. I was
frightened by a mouse, but what was most scary was this un-
sanitary, sedentary life without a house. With stains of dirt on
my shirt, face, knees and waist, I can see in the dream that my
life is a waste. The scenery was uneasily a grave wave of penury, where people, unbelievably, frequently live unequally.*

*I felt the tolling cold of a rolling river and couldn't control
the jolting shivers. It was at that coldest moment that I noticed
I was in a dream, and then focused my motions to awake and
escape my fate—a deteriorated state—upstream."*

As if under a spell, she was speaking to herself as she was
grieving for herself. Upset over how far she had fell. Wishing
she were somewhere else, with someone else, who cared and
was worth being held.

The jerk drove Jane to his place. To say it was an utter dis-
grace is an understatement; it was incased in the distaste of a
defaced basement.

Jane took one look at the house and couldn't control her
mouth. "C'mon, man… You tall as hell! I thought you were in
the NBA. That was just *game*?"

"I am. I am. This is where I stay to lay low," said the jerk, raising a hand towards the house. "You know, my safe zone… from all these crazy hoes."

To think, she was a perky, quirky little girl who loved Bert and Ernie. Now she's being coerced by a surly, unworthy jerk in her early thirties. Jane was skeptical, but still scaled the steps as she held the rail up to his less than acceptable dwelling. But her brain strayed and raced as she began to pray that there was some way to celebrate, rather than waste, her remaining days as an appreciated lady of patience and grace.

As a nightwalker, when her water broke she faltered, and revoked the hold on her daughter. She was thinking of her baby now, and how maybe now she could lower the inner torture as a talker on the altar. "I'm miserable. I need a miracle," she said in a low voice—not coy, only annoyed. But she kept poise, hoping to fill a void, and avoid being paranoid. Although, as if given clairvoyance, she did sense an impending ploy, possibly involving poisons and coitus, so she thought about her choices.

Normally, any opportunity to desert her dirty bird perch would thrust Jane headfirst into her expertly learned handiwork—jerk and slurp to quench her dying thirst to burst her purse with dough, sign paperwork to her own home, exert reserved perks and sport fly shirts. But to her own astonishment she blurted alertly, "I'ma try church!"

"What?" asked the jerk, clearly irked.

"You heard me," said Jane. "Searching for purpose, I been twerkin' since I was burping, but it ain't working... Only hurting. So I'm gonna try churching."

Before he could reply, she lowered her eyes and said, "Goodbye," petrified but excited to try a new life. She let her legs set the next step—leaving him perturbed, then turned and strolled along the curve of the curb, disconcerted but encircled with a churning current of courage. It was as if she finally realized that there is an hour when our paralyzing fright and anxiety of society's outline must be set aside and left behind with vises to find our guiding light.

Thinking about her knocked out on the couch waiting to be raped, he became outraged and felt as though he had been outplayed. Mouth agape in disbelief, the disturbed jerk screamed down the street, "Bitch, go to hell!"

Without turning to face him, she answered his terse curse, "Who needs hell when you've got earth?"

Writhing knights, like lions, have a fiery desire to bide time to fight for their pride, despite the tiring hide of iron they abide and the crises with which they've decided to collide.

Risk

It's now Tuesday, and his Mrs., and kids too, may soon miss Nick, considering who he intended to rudely misuse, and the tragic acts to ensue.

Someone Nick knew from younger had become an upper ranking drug runner for one of the city's biggest hustlers. To repay an old favor he simply gave Nick the hustler's number, under the guise that he was a wise juggler of hundreds of customers. What he didn't surmise was that Nick would be his supervisor's biting kryptonite.

Once in possession of the local mogul's disposable mobile, Nick left an impressive, precious message. One with no suspicious questions or aggression, and didn't demand a personal session. With such an impression, Nick fooled Slick Rick—the community's bigwig pusher, and pimp, too—into convincing his not-so-prudent lieutenants that Nick was an unruly tenant but a stellar seller. One who needed to bring a load of bills to close the deal on three pounds of unique, trendy greens with no seeds, sticks or stems.

When the conceited Slick conceded, Nick succeeded, and was given expedient entry to disobedient deviants—the pimp's most convicted, yet rudimentary, sentries. Based on what was conveyed, they knew Slick gave the okay. But it was only a ploy to adroitly destroy the loyally employed users of steroids, Roy and Floyd—who resembled coiled gargoyles, and roiled and annoyed the local dope boys like bad boils—then enjoy, like so many past royals, the spoils that follow recoil and turmoil embroiled on remote soil. With the quickness of an addict's twitch, Nick intended to pitch a few singed hollow-tips through the two menacing goons in a blitz.

***

As planned, he scanned the room as he advanced. When given the chance, he quickly gripped his cannons in his hands. He drew to shoot, and just as soon, seven lead heads sailed through the room to impale two males. At his left ACG, ACP shells fell like little brass bells, or the steady knell of heavy sledge hammers hitting nails on a rail.

With the rapidity, yet agility, of a vet, he met the threats as separate silhouettes to suppress. However, these silhouettes were blessed with the best Gazelles, sweaters, leathers and vests, and sat at a desk that was a pathetic mess but held a chess set that was just reset. One of the roughnecks was well-read; he left his TEC—the weapon he selected to protect himself as well as Slick's wealth—next to several texts on a shelf.

Nick didn't expect the hit to be uncontested, but they were more obsessed with flexing their pecs than correctly checking guests before letting them into the complex. Before they fell, the well-dressed transgressors regretted their misstep of easy access. They felt hell propelled from parallel barrels, smelt their apparel melt, bled, but never begged, though both boys yelped and flailed as the deck of death was dealt. All quelled, only a redbird was heard pecking at insects on a decrepit flow-erbed on the ledge, seemingly having leapt up from the hedges expressly to manifest some aspect of protest.

It was all executed to rip loot loose from one of two se-cluded pill-and-brick rooms hidden in the forbidden Linden tenements, where bookies, crooks and whores who flocked the block knew that these were not doors to knock on or come to. But Nick didn't flinch when he listened to attempts at intimi-dation. Nevertheless, the deft architect of theft jetted before getting arrested.

His guess that the meth chefs kept a heft of bread was cor-rect. After their inner clocks' tic-tocs and Nick's clips stopped, he made off with a suitcase filled with 200k.

Trying to keep his cool, he kept his stick shift coupe at a smooth cruise. Now poor, he could no longer afford a four-hundred-horse Porsche, so he settled for a Ford. It was used, maroon, and had been around for too many moons, but it still made it from A to B, and it was damn near free.

Hopes and dreams stave off suicide and save lives. If they were to die, so would we who strive.

Fitting Siblings

Nick's next move was to visit his sister, who sniffed and blew much more than the bubblegum she chewed. Unfortunately, there was so little Nick knew. She even stripped on cue in countless venues, for bouncers and chicks too. When the music and mood grooved, she had the smoothest dip, flip and spin moves. On her shin was a tattoo of a cute kitten cartoon with two balloons. And she was smitten with a caboose that left men consumed. Truly a considerate and gifted girl, but would spill lewd lyrics from her lips when you sipped booze, and blew piff, too, if you slipped a few bills through her thin swimsuit.

Known as Trixy to those who roamed the streets scorned, she was born Patricia—Trish for short. An enigma with charisma, she dreamed of chinchillas, and villas in Anguilla.

Her role doing rolls on the pole kept the Leo toned, and gave her sole control over her so-called grown goals, but extolled a toll on her soul that drove home a hole that strove to be consoled. Wasn't broke, so she no longer stole. She bought her own clothes, colors for her toes, cappuccinos, and blow for her nose. But even as her skin tone shone with a halo's glow and a bright white smile was shown as she spoke, she felt as though she was all alone.

While feeling disposed, she was cajoled—pursued and wooed with gifts and jewels by a shrewd tycoon. Now she was in the house doing as he chose. As if she were a Poodle or Bugle, her every move needed the brutal pimp's approval. But she eschewed to sit and stew, cooped up on curfew, with a limited view, and minuscule virtues, drenched in perfume and wishing to be rescued. Her single relished respite was sipping gin with spliffs and consuming pills and 'shrooms, as the continual bickering brewed. When they argued, he often left her bemused, with a chest of proof—even her tits bruised, when her skin hue switched blue.

After too many afternoons fraught with abuse in his loft, she was pissed and exhausted, and sought to risk the daunting cost of crossing the insolent boss, hauntingly, in an incident that involved his balls. But for her plan to succeed, she needed the scoundrel's arousal.

The soured flower jumped out of the scoured shower and stumbled into a towel. Patiently, she waited in a negligee and lace lingerie that accentuated her shameless shape, to manipulate her heinous prey into taking her persuasive bait.

She surely wasn't the first immature girl to be lured from her mama, assured by the provocateur of tours of the Bahamas and Tijuana. As daunting as an anaconda to an iguana when drinking vodka, he beat Rhonda, Yolanda and Shonda like he was E. Honda, and called them all prima donnas for their mani-pedis and sitting in the sauna. They were bound to live under his dogma, simply for moving them from Botswana and Uganda to a Ramada in Nevada. Haunted with the saga of drama and trauma, they consumed guava and lasagna infused with marijuana for an escape into nirvana.

Just as Trixy guessed, on this tipsy, whiskey-filled night, enticed by her appetizing thighs, he traded the attraction of lotion and napkins for her potions of sexual satisfaction on satin. He flattened out and unfastened his extravagant fashions. She was grasping and wagging his phallus with passion when he started gasping. "Yes, less nagging... I've been asking for more gagging," said the plastered bastard, grabbing her hair at the back, smashing her head into his lap. However, she didn't lick but bit the rude pimp's pruned prick, shooting excruciating agony, the likes of ten cavities, throughout his anatomy.

Eyes closed in anticipation of an erection, he didn't expect the infraction and had an erratic reaction—begging for a blessing with yelling that was deafening. "*Shhhit*!... Goddamnit!... You *fuckin'* wench!"

After settling, hesitantly, and seeing that there was no threat of his pecker severing, the guru, Slick Rick, sent troops from his crew to sentence what he assumed to be a stitch-inducing witch with a broom—because he couldn't view the wickedest bitch doing what she did in that room—to the crudest, grueling disciplining. These were hard-hitting, big brutes, minimum 6-foot-2, easily amused and skilled in jiu-jitsu—lethal moves used to bruise and split sinew.

They caught Trixy trying to catch a cab on Atkins Ave. The three commenced to kicking ribs loose with six shins and twelve-inch shoes. She spit mucus, drooled, and spewed pools of fluids. She kissed fists until her tooth slid from its roots. The pistol whipping split her swollen nose and lip, spilled hemo-globin all over her clothing. When they drove away boasting, she was approaching croaking. An old lady walking her shih tzu refused to intrude. But she did call the boys in blue.

In pursuit of a slick-suited gent to get hitched and spend her honeymoon with on a cruise ship, Trixy was tricked, controlled and misused. A few trips to Tiffany's on Fifth and some fits to look cute in, and maybe a 'Baby I miss you,' were not worth all the shit she went through. Now to fix her wrist the physician will need to use screws.

After this test and lesson, she would never again be so des-perate for affection. For as long as she lives, she'll be awaiting something real, and sincere, that she can hear, taste, and feel.

Due to my opaque hue, in chains I was exchanged to maintain the plains of grain and sugarcane on the grange of a new estate.

Slave to the Game

To guarantee he would remain as free as the beaked species, Nick chose to lay low in a cheap suite he deemed he'd need for about a week. By his estimation, by separating himself by at least three states, he had the leeway to evade restraints and a cage before the police could place and reach his location. The designated space was prearranged with a prepaid Visa in a fake name. A reservation made for the accommodations by one of his best mates, James, a friend since sixth grade who knew what was at stake without an explanation.

Nick paired chairs to barricade the place in case of an attempt to infiltrate. For the anticipated maid, a notice to not investigate or invade was displayed.

After a late look at the day's claim, he laid his head on a bed freshly made. No one pursued in his rearview, and the news had no clues, so the aloof recluse chose to remove his waterproof boots and snooze.

He mumbled but slumbered like lumber under a rumpled but fluffy, plush comforter. Then suddenly, before he was set upon and punished by an interrupting sun, he tussled as muscles struggled like the stutter of a discovered adulterer. A short, sharp shake and he was awake.

Nick was plagued by, and afraid he would never evade, pervaded and profane nightmares. Peaceful sleep was scarce, like waiting in the sleet, snow and slush for a bus that's slow to come, or longing for a terminus hug from a lost love who mugged you of trust but was once the snug socket for your monogamous pocket plug.

On occasion, his scares he shared with the rare few who cared. Like most others, the latest he would replay for his mother. He thought about the uneasy face she made when he said he had to leave and go back east. She was cutting onions, seated with bare feet, to give her bunions some rare relief. Nick felt she wanted him to live in a bubble. But to her, the jungle spelled trouble.

When he was expelled, in a cell in need of bail, and now in this motel, he could tell that his mother, Adele, of all personnel, didn't want him to fail. He had no hesitation in relaying to a stranger that when he was near danger, on occasion, he could hear his mother's exhortations. *"Be careful, don't cut your finger." "Don't bump your head, there's a board there." "Slow down, it's slippery out." "Be careful on that ladder."* And she was present for him to vent—without passing judgment—when he was knee-high in Levis, and now that he's grown. She picked up the phone with a groan in a low tone. In spite of being tired, she was excited and inviting.

"Nick? How you doin'?"

"Hey, Mom. I'm okay. How are you?"

"I'm all right. Just a little tired. What's going on?"

"Oh, I'm sorry. I woke you?"

"No, it's okay. I'm about to get up now anyway. Fix some breakfast or somethin'."

Nick sighed. "Oh, okay."

"So what's going on? You called this early I know it's for a reason."

"Just another bad dream. But this one was kinda crazy, actually."

"What happened? What was it about?"

"I don't know. It was as if... it was me, but it wasn't me. Like I was someone else in my dream. Maybe at some other time... in the past. You know?"

"Yeah, I know what you mean," replied his mom.

"Well, it was dark," said Nick. "Out in the country. Late at night." He began to describe his dream as if it was right before his eyes:

"Slouched, I crouch, denounced under a pronounced moon in June. With profuse amounts of blood, my mouth floods. In

tears, my spouse presses our weeping young near her breasts. Covered in mud, they tug at my lover's blouse and dress. They were conveying wails as if facing a killer whale or wasting away with caterpillars in a well. Their faces were smeared with beer, feces and fear. Their disgraced father dismayed and displayed in helpless distress.

The legitimately permitted hitting and beating in excess is merciless. Old frayed ropes in tangles are bound around my wrists and ankles. Tied between twin trees, I'm whipped. As I bleat and bleed, I bite my lip till it's ripped. A thick slit is split in the sun-stiffened skin of my ribs. Snaring leather is tearing and wearing muscle from tendon, tendon from bone. Each breaching, thrashing lash I screech, moan or groan. Mentally, I'm frozen in my own zone, stone-cold and alone, a solo stolen token below the potent blows of soles and elbows from emboldened, gloatin' foes.

In the sudden rain, I squeal when I feel surreal pain. Under the drummin' of thunder, I shudder and shiver. My gut, my liver and both lungs deliver a slow quiver. It grows up my throat and rises through my nose and eyes. I'm all choked up and broken inside. Despite my innermost spoken hopes and lies, I know it's as nigh as my sobs and sighs—this might be the night that I die.

The ropes I bore from the oaks are broken. Sinking to my knees, I plead for this mistreatment to cease. Beseeching some

man, or god, to render mercy. No grand defender descends.
No friend extends a hand. The excuses for these bruises, I do
not understand.

When I feel, for a perplexed moment of atonement, that I'm
blessed—that my upset oppressors are possessed by my re-
quest to ease this vexing stress and let me rest—what is done
next in disrespect I can't even digest. No less than wet tar is
tossed on the scars of my back, neck and chest. Screaming like
a siren from the increasing violence, my voice rises then dives
into silence. I lose control due to my injuries. Roll and kick
furiously until I am delirious. But these men are insensitive to
seeing the secretions from my eyes, and the saliva from my
teeth, mingled with the soil and oil spilled beneath my knees.

The third act to occur for my err is absurd. I recover to
discover I'm covered with birds' feathers. Tied to a tree with
my feet tethered together. Then they light a torch to scorch all
fight from my core. And end my plight with this deplorable horror.

Set afire, I gnash teeth and release a bleak shriek. Cheeks
so weak from screams that I can't speak. Crazed, going insane,
from the pain of this blaze, I gnaw at my tongue and jaw, trying
to erase my face.

At the pace of light, thoughts and sights raced through my
mind:

All of this for reading books?

For fleeing for freedom on foot?
Because I wrote a note about the vote?
And refused to use their god to keep me afloat?
Because a man died who denied me a decent life?
Where on earth hangs such a dark cloud?
How can this much hate be allowed?
Where a child is sold at birth...
 And her color is a curse.
I lived only to work, and worked only to live. Of another
man, I was the property. My wife, my children, not even they
belonged to me."

"Strange, right?" asked Nick. "It was like... I was a tortured hostage, in bondage. To my dry cries... no one responded."

His mother was moving around her kitchen, picking out in-gredients. "That is strange. Very strange. And it sounds pretty scary. I'm surprised you didn't wake up sooner. Try to shake yourself out of it maybe?"

"It's hard to," said Nick. "I know some people, when they realize they're in a dream, they can control it, or stop it. But I can't really do that. Plus it seems so real when I'm in it. What do you think it was about?"

"Well... maybe you're a slave."

"A slave?"

"Yeah, a slave in another way. Maybe you're a slave to the game." She held her breath.

"The game?" Nick asked in shocked disbelief.

His mother exhaled. "You know what I'm sayin'."

"Ma, what do you know about *the game*?"

"More than you think. Chasin' fast cash, and that mundane street fame... from cocaine. Only thing you really gain is a early grave or a cage," said his mother, then added, "and chains. That's why... honestly, I pray you've finally changed. I really do."

"I know, Ma. But I have changed, a lot, primarily for my wife and kids. Because of them, *and* you, I really don't wanna get locked up. But I won't lie, it's hard... just strugglin' to get by every day. Trying to take care of them, and myself?"

His mother had taken a seat. "Just take your time. Take it one day at a time. Ya know? Try to take it easy. It'll be all right. And please don't worry about me. I don't want you to do anything that might get you in more trouble."

"Okay, Mom. I'll just chill. Try to relax. Hopefully things will get better soon."

"Have you heard from Patricia?" asked his mother.

"I haven't. I haven't seen or heard from Trish," said Nick. "It's been awhile. I wanted to go see her if I could get in contact, but somethin' came up."

"Call me if you hear from her. I just been worried. Or have her call me if you get her new number. The one I had isn't working."

"I will," said Nick. "I'll call you. But I gotta go, mom."

"Alright… Just be careful. I love you, son."

"I know. I love you, too, ma."

"Okay. Bye bye, Nick."

"Bye, mom."

With plans to sail derailed, some stand still in hopes to prevail,
for eventually the raging hurricane will drain of rain and hail.

Searching for a Hurt Heart

Nick sniffed around like a sifting hound for two days straight, but found no account of pretty, but gritty, Trixy in town.

She had been running the streets, adjusting to hunting in the jungle to eat, for nearly three years. Coming from blushing and thinking sucking was disgusting to jumping in anyone's car and crushing, she sulked, huffed, and sunk into a funk, but did any stunt for funding from dawn to dusk. Crescently breasted and elegantly bowlegged, with perfected suggestive and poetic nestling and petting, she wasn't begging, and seldom disrespected by the pathetic men she was bedding. Although, dejected, she dreaded she would never see a wedding. And wrestled to make the detested day she was molested less upsetting.

Before she stirred on a sturdy gurney in need of emergency surgery and a firm attorney, the curvy girl journeyed assertively to the murkiest adversity, through the ever-deepening tunnel of the concrete jungle, amid Nick's most recent bid. Looking in the mirror, with no paternal fixture or father figure, and then no tender, bigger brother either, his bitter sister couldn't think of a better future to consider than attempting to get rich within the glimpsed imprints of constricting tricks and pimps.

On the prowl, around gnomes and cobblestone, and under the roaming eyes of owls and other fowl, Nick was now home and holding chrome. For nine months he was unconfined. He only saw his sister twice, but it was nice to vibe and get advice about life, rights, vise-tight vices, and even prices for white.

Now that his financial situation made a substantial graduation in such a short duration, he hoped to help her cope, relieve her load, and bring her in from the cold. In his bones and in his soul, he felt it was the least he owed for leaving her alone.

Behind closed doors, he dealt with deep remorse; he knew that him being sent up north was the source of his sister's current course. Enormous but physically formless, his love for her was like a gorgeous chorus.

Unable to locate Trixy, Nick thought the logical option was to check the jails' and hospitals' chronicles. He finally prevailed, and was able to exhale, when the operator gave veiled details about her lengthy stay for ails in Brookdale.

His temper simmered as he pictured his sister injured, praying she wasn't disfigured. As he pondered, he could nearly see her weak posture watched by doctors. But he refused to conjure an image much darker, for nothing would bother him harder than her departure.

***

Nick became weak and began to weep streaks down his cheeks at Trixy's feet—tucked under creased and pleated sheets—when he saw her unspeakably beaten features. He placed a cute bouquet and blue vase in a space by a gray tray displaying a baked potato with flakes of tomato, cake, and mango.

Even as she slept, she could hear Slick's steps coming up the stairs. The fear that he was near kept her aware. Some nights she just stared at the ceiling as tears rolled into her ears.

Pleased to see his baby sister whole, Nick squeezed her toes and poked at her nose. She awoke and not a word was spoken for a moment. As if they had seen a ghost or noticed someone who was stolen long ago, they were both stunned numb. Nick broke the rust from his bolts and plunged into a hug; she jolted, then posted to return the love.

A few minutes passed when Nick asked about the clash that left her with scabs, a cast and a gash. Then they discussed the unjust hustling pimp.

"How long were you seeing him?" asked Nick.

"Like six months. I didn't know his ass was crazy though," said Trixy, rolling her eyes.

"That's how it starts out; all good," said Nick.

Trixy became irritated and defensive. "Well, I didn't know he was gonna be on some, 'You ain't doin' nothin'. You ain't goin' nowhere,' type shit."

"I know. I'm not blaming you, Trish."

"So, do you know 'em?"

Nick wanted Trixy to relax, so he didn't chat about the fact that he too had crossed paths with Slick, or at least two cats that he worked with. "Not exactly. But I'll get to know him. Don't worry about that, I'll take care of it. I promise."

Trixy made a face. "Okay. Whatever you say."

"Do you know where he might be?"

"Not for sure. Around the city, he's got at least four spots he sleeps in. I've been to two. He changes where he stays every few days. Tries to throw the cops off. And anyone else, I guess. And he's always taking trips in and out of town."

In turn, Nick learned how much she was hurting. "Are you in a lot of pain?"

"Not now, I'm kinda doped up, bro," said Trixy. "How did you find me?"

Nick leaned against the wall by her bed, reading labels on her meds. "I just kept looking. And asking people. After a couple days, I checked the hospitals. I didn't wanna think it was possible, so I waited. I just knew you were somewhere else. Not in jail. Or the hospital."

"My cell phone got smashed," said Trixy. "So I couldn't call nobody."

"Yeah, I tried calling you a bunch of times. I figured it wasn't working, broken, or stolen or somethin'. I was just hoping you were okay."

"After a week here, I am better. But I'm still not okay. I can feel it."

"I wish you had my number," said Nick, putting one of her pill bottles down.

"I did. I must've messed up a couple digits."

Nick grinned and reminisced. "I remember when we were kids we had like a hundred numbers memorized. That's crazy, right?"

Trixy replied in kind with a smile. "Yeah, you're right."

"Wasn't no cell phones then," said Nick.

"Paper and pen," said Trixy. Then they both said, at the same time, "Right?"

They had a laugh on the path down memory lane. All the same, they were still in pain.

"Well, I'm so glad you came," said Trixy. "I was hoping you would. I didn't know how… but I kept hoping you would."

"If I could, there's no way I wouldn't," he assured his sister.

"Thank you. I'm happy to hear that. I really am."

Nick was still thinking of their childhood. "You ever look back and think about how it all went by so fast?"

"Yeah. But I'm glad. I hated my past."

"It wasn't all bad. We had some laughs."

"Yeah… we did," said Trixy. "But it was mostly a sad ass path. I had a father who was a part-time crook, part-time junkie. And a mother who rarely spoke to me, and seemed to only be concerned with her next lowlife boyfriend. How many losers did she drag in when we were growing up? Nine? Ten? Maybe if she had done a better job parenting her little girl, guiding her, preparing her, teaching her, then maybe I wouldn't keep finding myself in these fucked up situations to begin with. But she was on drugs or drunk when I needed her most. Oh well, the damage is done. I guess it's all on me now. Damn, life sucks."

"I'm not trying to make an excuse, but she wasn't raised right herself, Trixy."

"Maybe you're right. And I guess she had her own shit she was dealing with."

"Hey, it might not seem like it, but there were some good times… Do you remember water-balloon fights, or catching fireflies all night?" asked Nick, trying to cheer his sister up. "And what about hide and seek… climbing trees, playing dodge ball, or foot-racing kids down the street?"

Trixy began to reflect as well. "I remember jumping rope with my friends. Double-dutch. And hopscotch. Just running around outside having fun; I do miss that. Piecing old bikes together and going for rides was nice."

Nick became excited as he saw his sister's eyes light up and come to life. "Exactly! See, it wasn't all bad. Don't get me wrong, I know a lot of shit *was* fucked up. But… there are *some* times I wish we could get back. Simpler times."

Trixy was twisting the wrist that was still intact, as if it were stiff. "That is a fact; it wasn't bliss, but as a kid I did not see shit ending up like this."

Nick became concerned, watching Trixy squirm like a worm. "You all right?"

"A cramp," said Trixy, her hand clamped to the bedspread.

"You want me to get a nurse?"

"No, I'm fine," said Trixy, lying, then tried to make light of her strife. "It's this food; it's all bland. Anything with taste is banned."

"Did they say how long you have to stay?" asked Nick.

"They wanna keep me for another week. There may be more hemorrhaging."

"All right, that's not too long. It's best to be on the safe side. Hopefully everything's cool."

"Are you gonna stay awhile?" she asked her brother with pleading eyes.

"Yes, of course!"

"Good… good. I just need to get some more rest."

"Okay. Go ahead. Take your time."

"Love you, bro."

"I love you, too, Trish. Just relax. I ain't goin' nowhere."

"Thank you," said Trixy, with the sincerest gratitude.

She was lethargic from narcotics allotted for her hardship, having been swatted with carnage then discarded like garbage. But before she briefly, deeply departed, Nick, who took a lot of solace in her not being unconscious in the colossus hospice in Hollis, pulled a polished locket from his pocket and unlocked it. She watched in astonishment as he deposited the symbolic charm, fashioned as a heart for compassion, around her arm. Then he kissed her forehead before she swore about her soreness then laid her staid head back to rest in the bed.

Nick pounced down and lounged on the couch. With a scowl and a growl, he vowed aloud that the profound foul would not be allowed; that the coward, Slick Rick, would get disemboweled.

Like Siamese peas in sync and highly timely, the Pisces dreamed of unsightly scenes in the nineties. Feisty teens were fighting nightly beneath pricey Nikes tied around power lines and street lights to earn stripes for being grimy, while screaming "G.D." or "Almighty," in G.I., where wide-eyed, sheisty fiends might steal naïve tykes' bikes, clean and wipe all night, or hike miles in spite of it being icy outside just to ignite their life-stymieing pipes.

In wine-defiled eyesight, the precisely aligned city skyline shines with a slight likeness to the bright prideful lights of the time-divide supplied by the divine up high.

Home

Nick dialed his wife at five while driving to say he was alive and would arrive around nine. Though he didn't give hints about the risky hit over the phone, they spoke often after he smote those bozos like a virtuoso, stole their dough and chose to stay on the road and lay low. He mostly wanted to know if he got spotted—if cops were on the block watching his spot around the clock to get the drop. His wife—an avid ally and placid alibi—did not spot cops or a swath of SWAT, and they did not stop to knock, nor did she perceive anything odd, just a team of teen jocks, who rocked socks with flip-flops, nonchalantly mocking one of the lot for opting to don crocs, so Nick eagerly agreed to leave the cheap suite where he was presently, but irregularly, sleeping.

Nicole would never abort her support and report to court for a reward. Before giving birth, she was always onboard to consort in transporting scores of coke—commonly called 'weight' or 'work'—from ports towards the sort of folks who could afford to snort on resorts. And she still stood strong, surfing the storm, when her honey and the chubby lumps of slum money were gone, leaving her home alone with the kids as he did a bid. Sometimes fussy, but she sent her gully hubby money monthly and spoke on the phone lustfully. And she's been there since, swimming against the wind with no wins when it didn't make sense. It's a matter of fact; Nick's queen clings to her king like Reynolds Wrap on sticky rat traps.

Now that Nick netted his biggest score, he hoped to open his own domestic store. He was indebted to his wedded wife and cherished kids, who were destined to inherit the collected profits and benefits. After all, for years they bawled, so he owed it to them to now draw, and stay within, the lame lane of the law.

***

When he showed at home, with the undertone of smoke on his Colts overcoat, Nicole was solo on the taupe sofa, sober but sipping a mediocre mimosa, clothed in only a mocha kimono robe she wore to yoga. It was dim in the living room, where the simplistic lyrics of The Stylistics, intense incense, and alluring perfume loomed. On the mantel, she had candles lit. In the kitchen were biscuits and brisket in a skillet. And it must've been hours now since the little ones were hugged and tucked under comfy covers with tons of mom's abundant love.

As Nick was locking the top of the door, Nicole was trotting across the floor, her core throbbing more and more, now that he was there in human form. For the comfort of close contact she was starving—her desire a wildfire, carving a trail from her tail to where her limbs started parting.

"Baby," was Nicole's first word spoken, followed by a show of devotion, "I was hoping you'd be home this evening. I haven't been sleeping."

Her arms circled the surface of his bald dome like converging serpents, as her robe flowed and fell open, exposing golden globes made from a mold deemed perfect, though appropriately immediately broken.

"I missed you. A week seemed so long," Nick told Nicole, then kissed from her mint-dipped lips to her lobes. With the power to startle the most army-hardened sergeant as they sparkled, he marveled at her light-brown marbles.

With a hurtled implosion of emotions, an eternal, internal inferno girdled the Virgo's whole soul, proclaiming that all was condoned. Below her rib cage, holding her slim waist, Nick traced her rich skin with strength and grace. His fingertips found and fondled a thick, but fit, familiar figure of peaks, valleys he'd sallied with savvy, and cheeks. She felt weak between her hips, melted like cheese in his grip. Once stripped, he picked her up and took her on a quick trip to lay her godly body down and softly make her stir and purr naughty sounds.

From the dresser to the bed, like velvet feathers, her legs spread as if no lesser than a session in heaven was where they led. With her knees bent, she gingerly squeezed his stiff stick with the slippery grip beneath her recently cleanly licked clit, which piqued Nick's senses as if his nostrils and tonsils were steeped in a sweet, syrupy swirl of sugar and cinnamon. The cunnilingus was assiduous and generous—he considered her ticklish clitoris as delicious as luscious fritters or licorice.

As her heels lifted and shifted positions, he held her sinuous hips and healed her addiction, or had at least given her a fix, with his immensely missed gifts. It wasn't traditional medicine, but for his Mrs. it was of sufficient inches and had no comparison or precedent.

As the moon spilled into the room, his tattooed thews, exuding the fortitude of Cameroon, moved to the blooming cues of the mood. She had couth, but Nicole was no cold, mute prude when nude. Holding two in the womb, she had more than proved whom she would always choose, with all rules removed. Like the bluest tulip amongst putrid, polluted ruins, she was unique, rooted, and cute enough to seduce any dude, which included congruous students to the rudest users fluent in stupid.

As if warped to a vacuum or wrapped in a cocoon, there was exclusive focus between the two. Holding her close as further murmurs and moans of fervor rose, both were overloaded with an undertow of hormones as strong as comatose-potent methadone.

She split kisses betwixt his whiskers to whisper, with the hint of a whimper, "I miss you… I don't wanna lose you."

Under the influence of feminine juices suffused with soothing perfume and shampoo, Nick was a little confused. "I miss this, too. I mean, I miss you… too."

Nicole smiled at her boo. "We are like superglue; this duo is a union that no duel or dispute will ever loosen."

The heat between the two blew fuses. And after a brief reprieve to breathe, they dived deep into a repeat that exceeded belief.

***

He wedged and held her breasts as he slept. Nevertheless, being enmeshed in the sweat of the best sex didn't end his deeply recessed stress. While lying in bed, lies crept in his head. In the middle of the night, Nick woke and told his wife what he dreamed—that he was a hype for the ice, codeine and ketamine he once supplied to fiends:

"I sit and cringe as this thin, singed syringe signals me from afar. Shouting louder than any binge on gin I can comprehend

from a bar... I am immersed in adverse toils, as I converse with the worst spoil. Retrieval of the unequaled diesel in this needle leaves people peaceful and gleeful but feeble and leaning in the fetal needful of a sequel like Smigel. Eventually, I inched it into the skin of my shin...

I was another junky on the hunt for funds, just to get a bump to pump enough stuff in my veins to briefly alleviate my hunger pangs, leave my gums numb and my brain stained. It even relieved me of my own life's reins. More than grub, the vulva of a slut, or the comfort of a hug, my only love is to feel my blood flooded with this drug. I even infringed upon the gifts of my kids, sold their trinkets for hits in snippets as they winced and grimaced.

My eyes slide back in my head to unseen parts as the easing starts. I loosen my clenched fist when the soothing hits. As the vile blight of this vial fills my spine, my foul back feels so sublime. But this occurs for such a short time. This concise delight is not as serene as it seems. The price of this beguiling vice is quite high, like dice rolled for my life against rice. I am left with an icy sweat that feels like slime. Signs of more harm are the sores on my forearm. And I'm wrecked with regrets every night. I have no conscience or consciousness of consequences. Gruesome contusions, profusion of confusion, diminution of my pupils' visual acuteness, an urgent transfusion, and the removal of scruples are my crucial conclusion in the crucible of disillusion—"

Nicole assured him that it was only an impure, obscure dream, then demurely pulled him closer to feel as secure as sardines.

***

They didn't wake till late. When they did, the kids didn't hesitate to separate the drapes and place plates to taste the pancakes mom would make. Nick's mate created the greatest baked and braised meals, from a savory soufflé and marinated steak in paste to chilled veal, even charbroiled meat on the grill. Nicole hated waste but rarely overate, trying to maintain her weight and shape—without spanx. And she decorated their renovated cave in an ornate way. Infatuated since their first date, he rated her not as a ten or an eight but as more deserving of a cape than any lady to grace the Earth's face. But his wife was rightly a dime. Plus his bride couldn't be bribed to tell him a white lie.

For the sake of the race, it would behoove you to replicate their traits and relate to the way the faces of his family practically resonated placidly with the audacity of the galaxy. They embraced every day. And celebrated after days away. His soulful black family had a total lack of apathy. As loyal as gravity, actually happily hopeful, and social tactfully.

Nicole made Nick whole. So, he passed her half his salary every Saturday. He knew she was down like Mallory even in tragedy. His son, Ricky, was named in honor of his conquered father, who tried coke to cope and died of an overdose. He heard his spouse shout out loud about the worst birth pains when his baby girl came into this twirling world with a mane of curls. His final word on earth will be her first name, Tiffany—giddily prissy, so witty, and as pretty as a bitter-sweet symphony.

It was a shame, from so many days in the game, though he was scarcely afraid of being labeled a craven apostate, Nick was set in his caste ways, but didn't want the same for the babies he gave his last name.

He instilled discipline in his kids. And spoke to them often of life's options and toxins. They were expected to respect morals and values much more than mere valuables. Not to give in to trivial, material riches. Never burn their bridges, or get too big for their britches. Listen to bring their visions into fruition. And rather than pray that the pastor's answers for disasters, cancer or the hereafter, matter, walk softly not haughtily and covet that love and laughter make life lofty. He also taught with ample examples, so infrequent disagreements with his descendants didn't end in mistreatment.

For his kids, Nick would always take a break at home plate to play in snowflakes, skate, or wade in a lake. And he cherished his marriage before it was consummated; couldn't be baited to take the constellations as a consolation.

In reality, he unabashedly extended congeniality to the totality of his family. He had dozens of cousins, aunts and uncles jumbled in the struggle of the bustle and shuffle of the jungle. His dream for the team, currently, was to summon the humble in a huddle, then give them a couple of bundles of currency, as a courtesy, to obstruct their month-to-month stumbles and fumbled juggles.

After the kids ate eggs and pancakes, they made their way down the hallway to play. After being away for a week, the pitter-patter of their little feet made Nick's heart skip a beat. Replete with glee, they were unaware of their dad's illegal feats.

Once alone, Nicole strolled closer and probed. "So, why were you gone so long?"

Nick knew he had to chat with his better-half about the cash captured after blasting into lath and plaster through the two dapper crack traffickers' backs and bladders. "I was taking care of something for *us*. I'm sorry I didn't tell you in advance. I just didn't wanna get you involved. And if the cops came asking, I really didn't want you to know anything. I would hate for them to start talking that bullshit about an accomplice. Then threaten to take the kids away."

"You know I wouldn't say anything," said Nicole. "What, you can't trust me now?"

"Of course, I can. It's not like that," said Nick. "I just know it's better if you actually don't know anything when they start asking."

"Yeah, okay. All right. So where were you? Where did you stay?" asked Nicole, as she moved near the stove.

Of all the women he had known, Nicole was the most vocal, but also easily the most noble, love was her only and total motive, hence his proposal.

"I was staying in this quiet little motel. I reserved the room in a different name."

"You and who?" Nicole demanded, only half-jokingly.

"Girl, please. Anyway, I was making certain we would be straight for the rest of our days. I was too stressed to be trying to find some woozy floozies to screw in a Jacuzzi."

"Straight how?"

"Right now, in the car, I got a small suitcase with about two hundred thousand."

Nicole put a fist on her hip. "What*ever*. Yeah, *right*."

Nick grinned. "For real. I'm serious. Dead serious."

"A suitcase?"

"A small one, but yeah."

"Cash?"

"Yes!" Nick stated emphatically.

Nicole's eyebrows raised in surprise, with mesmerizing diamonds and sapphires in mind. "Let me see."

"Okay. Just wait. I'll bring it in in a minute."

"So how did you get the money?" asked Nicole. "Did you—"

Nick intervened, leaned in and seemed to beam as he began to speak of shooting the goons and relieving them of the loot. Nicole sat silent as her eyes widened. But she truly wasn't too surprised. Besides, she knew Nick tried to be the nicest, most compromising guy, but had done worse when penalizing conniving clients working on consignment. However, she was slightly frightened that he might be indicted.

"I'm just glad you didn't get hurt," said Nicole, sighing softly, as Nick took another sip of his coffee. "But baby, you have to think about your family."

"I *was* thinking about my family."

"Nick, you can't keep taking risks like this," said Nicole calmly. "It's too costly."

"I'm not. That's what I was trying to tell you over the phone; this is it. I was careful; nobody saw me come out of there."

Nicole took a seat, her shoulders suddenly heavy. "I can't do this again by myself—raising the kids. Crying all the damn time. Worrying about you..."

"So... now you're... ready to leave me?" asked Nick.

"No," said Nicole, her voice choking. "Though some things you do are terrible, my love for you is ineffable and irrepressible. You know that. But I couldn't handle your death. If you left, my heart would beat you to hell."

"Baby, listen," said Nick, "I want us to move."

"Move? Really?"

"Yeah, leave here. Leave all this mess. Too many bad influences here. Bad memories, too. We can go somewhere else and start over. Make some new memories."

"Are you sure you're ready for that? I mean, we've been here our whole life."

"Yes, I am. You're not? You're not tired of this? You don't think it'll be better for the kids?"

"Yeah, of course. Especially for the kids."

"There's just one thing," said Nick.

"What? What's wrong?"

"I stopped to see Trish."

"Oh. Okay. How is she?"

"In the hospital."

"Are you serious? What happened?"

"Some guys jumped on her. She got beat up pretty bad."

"Damn. I'm sorry to hear that, baby. Is she gonna be okay?"

"They think so. But I can't leave her like that."

"Of course, not! How much longer she gonna be there?"

"Maybe a week. I spoke to one of the nurses. Trish seemed to be very fond of her. Nice lady, but super garrulous."

"Do you know who did it?"

"Yeah, and that's just it—"

"What?"

"I don't know if I can just let it go."

Nick told Nicole his goals for the dough he stole. Then he spoke of his sister's gravely dismaying situation, and his declaration of retaliation. Nicole gave consideration to his burning determination, but persuaded him to make the observation that it was advantageous to wait for at least a short duration, until the implications of his latest violation were not glaring on the newspapers' front pages.

Nick finished his omelet then deposited the profit in the closet. He told Nicole, his goddess, that the smartest thing to do was to be modest—not to gossip—until they could leave their squalid streets like a comet-bound rocket, once the deed he promised had been accomplished.

It's commonplace to take a break to congregate and make your case in a debate as you patiently wait. Some see it as a relaxing vacation from their taxing occupation.

The Barbershop

What Nick witnessed in the hospital seemed impossible, but felt extremely colossal. Nicole, unnerved, concurred to be responsible for visits whenever possible, until the diabolical Slick Rick was targetable. To make that more plausible, Nick stopped at the shop for a novel's worth of the latest gospel. To avoid a debacle, he would seek to speak with the block's apostle—his barber at the parlor, Robert, who was keen on who was fleecing, grieving or meeting, whether cop or robber.

Far from squalor, the soccer watcher prospered as a proper barber. On occasion, he sweeps the accumulation of hair from beneath feet and chairs as patrons wait and read magazines, but he's a magician of precision, and as skilled with his instruments as any musician, using clippers and scissors to sculpt scalps into magnificent Caesars.

In his darker days as a mobster of honor popping lobsters and docking helicopters, he and his partner were monsters for the dollar. Not boxers, they were solvers with resolve who clobbered problems with choppers and revolvers. Robert was dubbed "Doctor Knocker," and his harsher friend, Dennis, "The Dentist," due to his acute intenseness.

Robert used to be a skinny hippie from itsy-bitsy, muddy, Money, Mississippi. He started out selling stolen cigarettes with his grisly, whiskey-drinking uncle Jimmy—a great tinkerer but not a good thinker. It was a pity, on the strength of a skimpy theory, Jimmy was swiftly proven guilty. Now it was nearly fifty years since his nephew moved to the big city. In a jiffy he went from petty theft to spiffy threads and enough credit for karats at Jared.

Doctor Knocker missed his friend, The Dentist, whose wickedness got him shipped out of the U.S. with little defense.

When the stork soared, Dennis was born to hold a sword, because his kin couldn't afford spoon nor fork. Moreover, they rarely ate more than porridge, and slept in a shed meant for storage. Therefore, since a youth, his views were distorted. The boorish boy soon aborted the boring chores he abhorred to consort with coke-snorting whores. He refused to be lorded over or accept living on a shortage. He had sordid dreams of importing portraits for his fortress, sort of like Gotti, with enough green, from a tsunami of Molly and Oxy, to buy Bugattis and Ducatis. Even if it took a heap of leaking bodies, eventually he'd be drinking kiwi martinis on the beaches of Tahiti or Fiji with sweeties in bikinis.

At twenty-four, with forged forms for America, he found an empty export ship at the port and boarded with his cohort—a whore with poor character named Erica.

Over the course of working in accord with Robert, he ignored laws of manslaughter, and resorted to assaults with scalding water. He went overboard because he swore someone was hoarding unreported dollars. His tendency to get pissed and flip his wig over the skimpiest diss wasn't a myth; with the swift swing of a scythe or a sickle, he'd send you to the crypt for a single twinkling nickel.

Smug and holding a grudge, Dennis didn't budge when the judge dropped the gavel and ordered him to travel—from a life indulged, plunged back into an insufferable time in utter drudgery and sludge. From court, the former poor farmer was escorted toward the airport to be deported for extorting drug lords for sport and reward through force. For thirty years, the dirty profiteer was an assassin with a passion for cash before he had his passport snatched.

A t The Barbershop, preachers, deceivers and retirees all link, sip coffee or tea, and speak equally with ease, while being cleaned neatly for meetings in eateries or simply to enjoy the city's scenery. Checking their necks' reflections, chicks get their sensitive kitchens snipped and trimmed evenly. Some seniors are here to have their head or beard sheared, some to hear their peers—coots who shoot the breeze and agree to disagree on sports analyses and expertise as they scream at referees on the T.V. screen. With a fresh cut and brush, young slick kids sit under a cape to get their seasick-waves shaped, and then leave to tease pencil-pushing, peasy-headed geeks just to be mean. And trainees appease cheap, conceited creeps pleading for freebies because a sneeze, or a peek at a sleazy skeezer crossing the street, left their lining leaning and zeeked like a 3D trapezium. But these employees' techniques are not backed by licensees or framed degrees. There are no receipts or guarantees for the displeased. In here, even police keep the peace. And there exists few distinctions between Buddhists, Muslims, Jews and Christians. The only truth was that everyone was free to visit, from hooligans and loose women to beauticians and schoolchildren.

Robert really bought The Barbershop strictly to keep busy. He was nine years retired from a glorified life of crime. He persevered in his career of racketeering, but merely became weary of adhering to his theory to be leery of everyone far and near, though clearly he was severely revered and feared, even by those who sneered and jeered at his rear. However, his ear was ceaselessly near the streets, to hear the creeping of thieves, dealers with keys, killers with heat, and the appointees.

He readily saw levity in his destiny as an elderly man of integrity, temerity, and clarity, in his seventies, without celebrity, but carefully invested equity. If done successfully, he would be living in serenity with a new identity, enjoying pleasantries and avoiding old tendencies. All after cleverly eluding enmity due to exigencies of enemies and deputies.

Considered incapable of fables, Robert's word was impeccably stable. A unique breed of O.G. who didn't repeat secrets, he was frequently seated as a neutral union between numerous dudes who intended to get business accomplished, with unfamiliar correspondents, without the sickness of snitches to bother them. If the swiftly shrouded Slick Rick could be found, Nick didn't doubt that Robert had the clout and scouts to find out the pimp's whereabouts, without it being touted by loudmouths. Besides, today he could use a shave with a straight blade that wouldn't agitate his face. It had been three weeks since his cheeks were treated to the sleek neatness of steam and cream, which was greatly favored over a cheap razor—like a mobile phone compared to a pager.

Robert was delighted to set sights on his friend. "Hey, man!" he exclaimed, lowering a client in his chair.

"What's good, old man?" Nick asked in a jovial tone.

"The hood, baby. The hood," said Robert, showing off his pearly whites.

"Shit, I wish," said Nick, simultaneously shaking Robert's hand and giving him a hug as though he was his long lost brother.

"How's the fam? I know Ricky and Tiffany are as big as the Mrs. now." Robert was dusting his chair—getting it prepared for the cutting of another head of hair.

"Yeah, they're sprouting up, man," said Nick, smiling proudly with his children in mind.

With no signs of contrite, the mighty barber kindly invited Nick to a tidy area to share his slightly reclined shiny chair. Politely, with an obliging smile, Nick skipped the line without a gripe, stare or swear from patrons patiently waiting to have their hair repaired or shaved bare.

On the tube, the news issued skewed clues as to an accused shooter who was on the loose. It was assumed that after his shrewd ruse of a crew, he slew two goons in a room used to distribute and hold kilos of dope. Always cautious of his environment, Nick gazed intently at every client, checking for changes in the current climate, but didn't fix his attention on anything specific.

Robert spread shaving paste on Nick's face, then traced the straightedge all the way to his neck—as if scraping waves from a hectic lake—erasing every speck. It was surprising how many guys didn't mind sliding under his knife. As a barber he was nice, but in his prime he'd hardly think twice before slicing your windpipe.

"Yo, Rob, you think we can speak in private for a few minutes? I mean, once you finish?" Nick asked his friend, who was getting bits of paste off his chin.

"Of course, man. You know I got *you*."

In the meantime, Nick put his concerns in the back of his mind. "So, how's business been?"

"I can't complain," said Robert. "We keep the regulars happy, so they keep coming back. And I haven't had to let nobody go."

"That's good. We all gotta eat," said Nick.

"Well, at least nobody worth keeping," Robert clarified.

"Don't tell me you brought in some knuckleheads again."

"You know me; I try to give everybody a chance. Sometimes a second chance. It's rough out here. *That* I understand."

"Yeah, we all got a past," said Nick.

"Including me. For sure," said Robert. "So, I try to show a little love."

"I feel you, but they gotta come correct though," Nick demanded. "I am not one to put up with people's bullshit."

"True that. Man, these young cats I try to get work for now… they think they deserve somethin'. *Just* for being born."

"I know the type," said Nick.

"They got no hustle," said Robert. "Not in school, sports, or even the streets. *Nothin'*. It's a damn shame."

"And ain't nobody gonna give you nothing. You gotta earn it."

"Exactly," said Robert. "I told this young punk, 'You work, you earn it, *then* you deserve it.'"

"Word. But too many of these cats are lazy, and they feel entitled."

"Just because they were born, huh?"

"A lot has changed."

"A lot remains the same."

"You right about that," Nick agreed. "But a lot of these kids wanna be bums. They don't want shit out of life. They like this ghetto stuff."

Robert took a step back and gave Nick a puzzled look. "We agree; too many of them *are* lazy. Ultimately, I blame the parents for that." Robert tapped a comb on his palm. "But do you really think these kids *wanna* be out here killing each other, robbing, stealing, selling drugs? You think they're okay with their moms and sisters living in crime-ridden areas? *Hell no!*" He shoved the comb back into his pocket, but now his hands were up and moving with his fingers spread apart. "Listen here, if they could change places with a kid who hit the lottery of life, who was lucky enough to be born into a somewhat stable middle-class family, they'd do it in a heartbeat."

"You sure about that?" asked Nick.

"*Shit* yeah! Some of 'em try to act tough, like they wouldn't switch places, but at the end of the day, they know what it looks like to have, and what it feels like to have not."

"You may be right. I guess a lot of them just don't see anything worth living and fighting for," said Nick. "Besides a gang, of course. And some gangbangers who they think might actually die for them, or even do life."

"First chance they get, they snitch," Robert stated, as a matter of fact, learned from experiences of his past.

"And if they don't they're up Shit's Creek without a paddle."

"All for some bullshit—a pistol, or trying to earn some street-cred or respect. It's stupid and silly. But it's also sad… Back in the day, our thing was organized, structured. None of this wild cowboy shit—shooting everything that moves."

"Sad is right," said Nick. "But they really don't give a fuck. They don't have anything to give a fuck about. Many of them don't see any hope or future. No light at the end of the tunnel. Just more of the same—poverty and struggle. Struggle just to have a little bit of nothing. And they're just kids dealing with this stuff. I know how it is. When I was young, I knew I would get snuffed. I couldn't see myself growing up."

"Kids killing kids," said Robert.

"I wish it would end," said Nick. "I guess you need to know the reason for it all, to end it. Each case is different."

"Each case may have some minor differences," said Robert, "but there's a lot of parallels with this tit-for-tat gunplay that goes on every day. And I believe it's due to a number of reasons."

"Like?"

"Well, for starters, living in a neighborhood like that, you can't afford to be passive; to be seen as weak is a liability. Throughout human history, many duels have taken place simply on the basis of disrespect. And, you don't have the means to simply move away. You live in a tough environment, which requires *you* to be tough as not to be repeatedly victimized, with impunity. And the people don't feel they can trust the police to protect them either. On the contrary, there is a long history of distrusting cops, for various reasons. Some legitimate, some not…"

"Right, some distrust *is* justified," said Nick. "I know a lot of people—innocent and minding their own damn business—who've been harassed, humiliated and degraded. If it wasn't for pride, it'd bring tears to your eyes. Police repeatedly interrogating and frisking you just because you're too poor to live somewhere else? It's bullshit."

"Oh, *I* get it. But back to what I was saying: If you *do* tell the cops about someone, someone *they* know may victimize *you.* Another reason for this tit-for-tat gunplay is, if someone feels threatened, they may think it's necessary to take preemptive action, in a way that law enforcement cannot. If they hesitate, or seek counsel or protection, they themselves could be the one killed. Then, there's the heartbreaking, depressing, but very much real fact that when you don't know anything else, as a young man, that type of life can be *tantalizing*, exciting, emboldening. They really need somewhere else to channel their angst, energy, and thirst for adventure. Also, many of them are very young, under twenty. They're not fully developed in a way that allows them to properly process the consequences of their actions."

"Yeah, it's just back and forth; you kill mine, I kill yours," said Nick, wistfully thinking of his own culpability.

"On top of all the despair, killing, and crime," said Robert, "they live in a country where carrots of comfort, convenience and luxury are constantly dangled in front of them. In a highly materialistic and media driven country, your self-worth is often associated with possessions. That works on the psyche of the poor just as much as anyone else. Maybe more so."

"I know what you mean," said Nick. "When I was out there hustling I definitely wanted a piece of the pie. At the time I didn't see, or know, any other way to get it but crime."

"That's a damn shame, man."

"But the truth."

"The unfortunate thing," said Robert, "is that these kids don't see the full value in themselves, or other people born into similar inauspicious situations."

"In-au-spicious?"

"Discouraging... ominous... unpromising," Robert clarified.

"Oh, okay," said Nick, gesturing for Robert to continue.

"Where they see the most value, and potential for success, concentrated, is in those persons whose lives look nothing like their own."

"White people," said Nick, with certainty.

"This is not just as simple as black lives and experiences compared to white ones," said Robert. "This is more so looking at and seeing the glaring differences between poor people, of all races, around the globe, and those who have some semblance of a decent start in the race of life."

"So... mostly white people, right?" Nick asked sarcastically as he tilted his head.

"Yeah, man, mostly," said Robert. "But trust me; more than race, money makes the difference. If you're poor, you're powerless. If these kids were rich, or just well-off, they wouldn't be going through all this shit. And if a rich, or middle-class, kid did commit a crime, or cheat, or lie, he's much more likely to get a slap on the wrist."

"Hey," said Nick, "I don't have a problem with *anyone* based on race. Like Dr. King said, 'I judge by the content of character, *not* the color of skin.' But the fact is, here *and* around the world, on *average*, white people *are* far better off. So, I was just making a point."

"I got your point," said Robert, and went on, "Now, where these kids live, in the ghetto, you have a high concentration of poverty. That concentration breeds hopelessness, desperation, and a strong sense of not belonging—as though this praised and paraded American Dream was never meant for anyone like them. Everywhere they turn, they see nothing but the same sad shit."

"I feel you," said Nick. "When you have a concentration of people like that—poor people, poorly educated, with little hope in sight—you are guaranteed to see those same people taking unusual risks for minimal reward, turn to crime, and hold a devalued idea of life. I get it."

Their dialogue got clogged with a fog of quiescence, so Nick interjected with a new subject. Because he respected Robert's intellect, he suggested something he often suppressed but could lead to a lesson or a confession. "Yo, Rob, do you believe in a god?"

"Now there's a peculiar question. A god, huh?" Robert asked, and then paused. "Why do you say '*a* god'?"

"Well, you know," said Nick, "a lot of people believe in different gods, that's all."

"Why do you ask?"

"Just thinking, man," said Nick, adjusting his posture. "Things I've done… Things I *might* do… Things about people I know."

"Me?"

"I'm not ya judge, brotha," said Nick, with a lighthearted grin.

"Well, let's see… I know in the Bible it says, 'God *is* love.' Therefore, love *is* God. Maybe there's some truth to it."

"That's interesting. I never heard that before. Never thought about it like that."

"Yeah, maybe because, some would say, love is, possibly, the strongest force you will ever encounter."

"You think so?" Nick asked with a raised eyebrow.

"Hey, man, out of love, for love, someone will do the impossible," said the barber, then continued, "Besides, I'm sixty-three years old, and at this stage, I'm not ashamed to say that a broken heart is an emotional and physical combination of compressed stress you don't dare readily repeat. It can mess you up, son. I've seen it done."

"I'll give you that, love *is* a force," said Nick. "But hey, you live and you learn and life goes on."

"Tell me about it," said Robert, after finishing Nick's shave and removing his cape. "I feel like... the love—the infinitely powerful affinity—for a child, religion, or god, has led people to do things—good and bad—that they wouldn't otherwise imagine. Or possibly even be capable of."

"Yeah... the risks we take."

"And that's just it; with love it's not seen as a risk. It's just..."

"The natural thing to do?" Nick offered.

"Yeah, you could say that. Instinct. Impulse, you know? In general, when emotions are involved, you can't be a hundred percent sure how you'll handle, or react to, certain situations."

"Well, I'm still trying to figure this whole thing out, old man."

"What's that?" asked Robert.

"Life," Nick replied.

"Here's a little secret," said Robert. Then, in a whisper, "We all are."

"Nobody said it would be easy, but nobody said it would be this hard. Wish I was warned from the start."

"Young man, you'll be fine."

"If life is kind," said Nick. "I don't wanna live just to take my next breath and eat my next meal. I'm trying to leave my kids a will worth at least a couple mill'."

"It's heavy. Life's heavy, son. You *can* get crushed... those of us not strong enough. It is quite a conundrum. But some things only life can teach."

After the shave, a perfectly paved face remained. Robert then led Nick to a larger part of the shop's locker room, where stacks of boxes were stocked along with brooms. Here, they could speak with no threat of regret—from secrets being leaked to the press by a pest via internet.

Nick prodded and mentally jotted imparted knowledge on topics from philosophic logic to narcotics. Then he alluded to his pursuit to subdue the elusive Slick Rick, and construed that the pimp's day to rue was due. Robert thought it ironic that Nick robbed the same demonic pimp who attempted to kill Trixy on the opposite end of the city. Nick's initial issue was if his friend knew a few of Slick's venues used to rendezvous. The bigwig definitely registered. Robert was aware of the character's irregular visits. He remembered him as a pedicured predator for secular women, who sipped spirits and insisted on an addiction with expensive gifts and linens, as well as being a creditor—with uninhibited limits—for amateur developers and embezzlers. He attributed this elicited wisdom to Slick's competitors' messengers. From the murmurs he heard, he learned

of a dilapidated Day's Inn eight miles outside the main inter-
state. A place Slick went with his earners—confirmed murder-
ers with burners who were certain to put in work—to personally orchestrate and tabulate trades of an array of weight for
pay.

When their collusion in seclusion concluded, Nick told his
bold old friend thanks for the information and the shave, and
then made his way to his musket-holding, rugged rust-bucket
out front.

Nature rarely creates the innately crazy and nutty—namely Gacy and Bundy—the inhumanely hungry, not for fame or money, but both the shapely and chubby, whether shady or bubbly, to cuddle as buddies then cover their bodies with gravy and honey.

Roger

Weaving between people while leaving the shop, Nick nearly knocked over someone he hadn't seen in what seemed to be a century. Realistically, it was a string of fifteen difficult springs in the penitentiary, to be horrifically specific.

Inquisitive, Nick said, "Roger," just intense enough to get the guy's attention.

"Nick?" The guy replied, with wild, wiry eyes, acquired from too many nights frightened for his life.

"Yeah, man. It's been forever."

"You still look the same, bro."

Nick was slowly moving towards his car. "You know black don't crack."

"I see that. I wish I could say the same."

"Hey, man, I gotta go before a tow truck shows up," said Nick. "But I'll check you later. It was good seeing you though."

"Yo, take my number. Call me when you can."

Nick's eyes tightened. "All right. Cool." What he was thinking was something totally different, *"Soon I'll move to the west where he won't be a threat."*

Nick suffered the buster's numbers without a stutter, but had no intentions of giving hints at his living conditions, his Mrs.' position or his children's school district. Nick predicted Roger was one to make victims of men, even so-called close friends. And within a fleeting week, if he wasn't remanded, he planned to advance to an expanse of financed land in the sand, as a voter of Arizona, holding a Corona or cola on a sofa, with the aroma of a smoker with glaucoma over toga covered shoulders. He didn't need the conflict of a recently released two-time convict as his new sidekick. He hit Roger with a rigid grip then left tread shredded as he sped off with a cynic's grin.

Nick was intentionally elusive; he knew Roger to be too intrusive. And besides being used for ruthless shootings, the nuisance was useless; a foolish man who made ludicrous excuses and blamed his accusers for his ruinous abuses at all of his rulings. If entrusted with the simplest clue, he would surely prove to be a real Brutus.

Just six to eight more days with no mistakes, and Nick would escape this underground game of fascists, like a Venus-bound Phoenix from flames and ashes; no more clashes with classless lames, leeches and backstabbers.

With a wanderer as a father, Roger was odd since a toddler. Far from a scholar, after the brawler's departure from his foster sponsors, he became a squatter, and was placed on police blotters for stealing copper and as a pickpocket of shoppers.

He was last knocked to rot, with three-hots-and-a-cot, for a botched robbery. With twin Glocks, he startled and robbed a McDonald's collar for the week's drop. The employee lobbed the dollars and peed in his socks. Hollering at joggers, Roger retreated up the block. But was shocked to meet the heat of three cops walking the beat. They did not get within reach to extend hands and apprehend the demented man before he sprinted up the cement and circumvented a rented van. He felt a gust of wind when a bus went rushing just within inches of crushing him. He threw the bag and a gat into a huge patch of uprooted grass and weeds beneath a tree, where he intended for them to blend in and prevent detectives from pinning him with evidence. Though he didn't get to spend a cent, the cops documented his offense and sent him in for a subsequent stint, after he was hemmed up and kicked in his tendons without relent.

He was dumb enough to dump one of the guns under a truck as it pulled up. A small-pawed dog gave the trucker cause to pause. When Roger was caught by the cops the truck pulled off, exposing the gun he tossed by the exhaust. The brunt of life's kicks in his nuts had come from being as dumb as dung.

Being represented as a defendant in detention had become his resented, but obviously not amended, trend. Roger previously did three for a B&E and larceny. Not to mention he swindled a brittle crippled man for his crystal. Though sinful, he was wishful for acquittal. They didn't get a conviction because the victim couldn't give a limpid description. He was afflicted with poor retention due to a dilemma with incipient dementia.

***

Hours elapsed fast like playing craps in a trap. While flapping at gnats, Vincent and Kenneth—two misbehaving, forsaken vagrants—located Roger's hastily stashed cache in the grass. By all but the grossest rodents, the stolen dough and loaded gun went unnoticed in the foliage. Out late craving a payday, the displaced kids were amassing smashed cans in a Glad bag—a gig propositioned by the persistent Kenneth, to keep the two cribless kids independent and out of prison until they could envisage a more sufficient system of subsistence.

Calm as a swan, Kenneth had no nagging qualms with hitting his friend's lacking palms, passing him half the cash and offering the chap a balm-sapped dap. But Vincent had to have both halves, since his hand grasped the gat. It was sad, but after years on the same path, in a habitat with famish crabs, Vincent was willing to end this impasse by detaching from his friend like wheat from chaff. Kenneth was hoping that Vincent was only joking. He was known to be a comic after choking on exotic chronic. But Vincent's gremlin grin was not of frolic but solely sardonic. A diseased creature in sneakers, besieged with evil, was revealed in his features—a slim Grim Reaper in a white wife-beater.

Friends since fifth grade, still he didn't hesitate to wave the steel in his face. Kenneth had one thought, "Abel ate and drank at the same table as Cain." He couldn't pray or dash, the outcast crashed to the grass as brass was cast out and flashed on the drab trash bag. The psychopath snatched the package from in back of Kenneth's ravaged cabbage and made for the passage of the underpass.

Unbeknownst to most, this wasn't Vincent's first murder; there was a precursor. Working as a burglar, he discovered an observer. He broke her nose with the phone's receiver and took a cleaver to his grandfather Peter's cleaner's femur, squeezed her in a mini freezer and hid it three meters deep near a Cedar.

A week passed before the greedy, weak savage clashed with Kenneth's unholy cronies and roadies. They branded and bashed the bandit with damage beyond bandages. His cranium was caved in with a cane and a bike chain. Rain came and waned later the next day, still pale blood stains remained.

Now that Roger was free, the creep wanted to finally critique real physiques and toes of freaks, not just those in videos or between magazines' sheets. So he went on a mission in a gentlemen's club for a solo show and audition—from an unwitting potential victim—amid women with less than ribbons on their kittens.

With idiotic alcoholics, the spot could get chaotic. It was a den of sin, where men spend Benjamins and get to grip a hen's uninhibited tit. Limber strippers thicker than Snickers shimmer with glitter in the mirror. Behind the filter of denim and zippers, dicks get stiffer than twisted pillars for typically physically exquisite ex-babysitters pivoted to explicit go-getters. They snicker, whisper wicked riddles, and give a little wiggle. The richer the bidder, the more they'll deliver, from a rub of your pickle to a tickle or jiggle of Skittles-sweet nipples. Fickle kissers, they lick glistening lips strictly for tips. In this den, the glimmer of a big tipper's ring on his wrinkled trigger finger gripping a pitcher can send skilled gold diggers into tingled fits, mingled with swivels and slithers swifter than Olympic swimmers, for a sliver of silver.

The stocky Roger had a habit of stalking women. Those who wouldn't lend him a minute to talk he fought, telling himself it was their fault. A frail-minded man who continued to fail and find his way inside a jail cell, he never dealt well with females. His only aim was to persuade them to lay with him. If he couldn't persuade them he raped them. Most were too afraid, or ashamed, to place blame. In one way or another, he left a lake of eighty ladies' tears cascading in his wake. Fascinated with degrading behaviors pertaining to inhumane constraints, the insane ape strangled some of that rain from an underage cutie he roofied back in the day named Jane.

From the pole, Roger focused on an ambrosial Creole with the bold eyes of a doe, whom he hoped to grope, to bestow placebos on his machismo ego and libido. As a bonus, he noticed the lotus was holding a grip. His hostess unfolded the roll of dough and slipped in more photos of old dead men. He told her he wasn't cheap and needed a seat in the V.I.P.

"Hello, beautiful. Are you free to play?"

"I'm not free, but if you're paying I'm playing."

"Well, I meant *available*. Anyway, what's your name?"

"Grace."

"No. Your *real* name," Roger demanded.

"I just told you, *Grace*. It works, so I use it."

"Well, look here, *Grace*. I can pay *whatever* you want, if we can get some privacy."

"Sure," said Grace, "that's no problem. No problem at all."

The girl was no slouch. In a used, wool blouse, nude, or in a full gown, she stood out in a crowd as if she wore a crown. From the playground she was stage-bound by way of Greyhound. Now her round, brown mounds vibrate in the night's shade for dehydrated, preying primates, to pay the valet—an ese from LA named José—an astounding amount of dough without delay for profound essays, or so goes the old cliché, "I'm only stripping to pay my way through school." It was more likely he endowed the pouty performers with pounds of powder to drown their snouts in.

What Grace became was truly a shame. If she had a little persuasion at an early age, she may be doing plays or ballets on Broadway today.

Her accent was melodic, harmonic, almost hypnotic. But in Roger's rotten optics was a not-so-methodic plot for a brisk economic swell. After several spells dwelling in a cell, the infidel's hunger for a carousel of hell wasn't quelled.

The quack slapped her tail as it fell in his lap and repelled. When she raised her ass, he swore he saw a gazelle grazing on grass. As she danced and relaxed, her rack glanced and tapped his fitted Packers cap. His cock throbbed as he watched the blonde's crotch with a Spock-like mindlock. But what he wanted to touch was her money-stuffed clutch. When she squatted erotically, the psychotic pulled a Glock from his pocket, put it to her armpit, then lifted the stripper's grommet-dotted wallet from a slot on the couch and darted. She followed and hollered for the guards taking gate charges and investigating dates on cards. In a Titanic-like panic, they took action to catch and banish the outlandish bastard, but to their disadvantage he managed to back up to a combative stance, then blacked out with a strap brandished in mannish hands, set to command an avalanche to supplant the impeccant and the damned, rather than get reprimanded and crammed back in the can. In seconds, his pistol was ejecting shells in quick succession like a wicked engine piston—pop pop pop pop pop pop pop pop pop pop. When the shots stopped, the Glock's firing pin had dented ten primers in; the entire clip had been expired, and nine innocents had been hit and lay dying as spent shells went flying.

As grim as the Apocalypse shielded in a full eclipse, the sight of the incident was stifling. Witnesses and survivors were hiding or trying to revive victims they could find. Some were left helpless, with wounds to the pelvis or intestines, as the selfish headed for the exits.

A faithful waiter's shoulder blade was grazed. Despite the abrasion, she made her way to the gun safe. She came from around the bar and appeared at Roger's rear, put a street sweeper to his ear and seared his fears of serving more years with disturbing peers. The buttstock kicked as buckshot was spit and another nut got hit. He was instantly skewered steak stuck with steel sticks in Lucifer's sweltering pit.

After seeing the chump's body slumped, one of the club's loveliest bunnies couldn't keep her lunch from coming up. Roger was laid flat like a stray cat. Chasing fat, gray rats across the tarmac got him smashed as if by a linebacker, a giant's axe, an unlicensed five-time-DUI driver in a Mack.

As a boy, he didn't have many toys, and he nearly never knew joy. For him, no one was likely to grieve, but he never had an equal opportunity to reach his full potential or succeed; his reality was steeped in fatalities, brutality and immorality since he was conceived.

Nestled in metal vessels crossing ponds and lawns with squads of
pawns called Devil Dogs, to wrestle spawns of demagogues, an about-face
was made on the job to be a cog in the clock of hogs.

Maniac

According to the gospel of Robert—the block's apostle—Slick's conclave of three acclaimed gangs had a set date of April 8th. If things went his way, in two days Nick would be there to initiate a devastating raid. His aim was to shake the place like a quake equating to Bane on octane, or insatiate flames scraping tanks of propane, then overtake and annihilate the room while the gangs are incapacitated by consternation and outrage, to ensure he escaped unscathed. If done in a suffocating way, half the inane goons in the main room will be sprayed and done away with before they can make a move. He wasn't interested in distinguishing between crews, only extinguishing anyone looming. To get to Slick, Nick was willing to kill every morbid and dimwitted misfit in the district. He was hell-bent on finishing his mission. But to accomplish this he needed better ballistic equipment.

To successfully aggressively infiltrate the dilapidated estate demanded preparation. That and the help of his main man Jason. But first he preferred to contact Mack, to get automatic ratchets with metallic brackets and combat attachments, the kind to establish a rib-rattling racket and cause the faction of maggots to inhabit plastic and caskets the fastest. Called ratchets due to the fact that they were used to tighten a few loose ends. Not the type of tools used to drive screws, but the kind utilized to rectify slights, snafus and abuses, by smiting impolite individuals and despised crews with which you might feud.

Bred by the streets when there was little bread to eat, Mack joined the Marines and became an exceptional professional soldier, not just a poser with a shoulder holster. Malnourished but filled with fervid courage, he flourished in the service, even when girded by a turret amidst the whirlwind of skirmishes. He worked over fourteen years in the Corps before he restored his twenty-four-hour rapport with the corner, which, according to the former warrior, was worth more than being a corpse in the morgue or on some foreign shore. He accumulated scores of accolades over a decade of campaigns with his brigade, but always felt unappreciated and underpaid. What's more, time away, plus his tryst with an escort, forced him into divorce. For all of his moral shortcomings, to Nick he was sort of a mentor, more so in matters of war.

Mack had two big, black tats on his back. One cackled like a jackal. The other wore a frown. Both were crowned clowns. The sway of his patiently paced gait and his frank gaze say he wasn't a saint, but he had saved men on several occasions, from Blacks to Caucasians, while fighting back Arabs and Asians, for his flag and nation. At his late age, he calculated it all as the selfish gain of a partly racist, largely snake-infested nation, where his great ancestors, because of hatred, were separated, discriminated against, and couldn't claim an equal place to bathe in. "A nation," he would say, "that is skilled at seamlessly changing from instigator to mediator, when playing state against state."

His killing skills were honed on fields far from home; fighting planes and tanks in strange places laced with Agent Orange, for minimal, trivial gains and that same nation's praise. As a baby-faced teen, a fake deal sealed his fate. The story told and sold to him was that of saving souls from Satan. Satan being any state that wasn't as great as his own U.S. of A.

When an aircraft was hijacked and used in the Pentagon attack, Mack and his comrades were tasked to pack the fat and flesh of men's backs into the feds' hazmat bags and clear the crash path in gasmasks. That was his last order from the Corps.

His nickname in the brick game was Maniac. He hated fame, but for sacks of cash he was a brainiac with class who didn't slack or lollygag. And as a reader of police procedures, he was keener than most blokes.

He came a long way from the little likable lad loving Little League, large libraries, learning Latin languages and linking Lincoln Logs and Legos. Once the local Pharaoh of the ghetto, thanks to a pact with his fellow, Pueblo, and a macho capo, Marcello, Mack now had the dinero to live mellow near meadows, sipping amaretto and Modelo under sombreros. From moving packs he had amassed a maroon and black Cadillac, a beige Range Rover, a condo close to the snowy slopes of Stowe, a townhome in Coconut Grove, and enough stacks to last well past his last grand kid's passing. At his level of success, getting possessions repossessed wasn't a stress. Nevertheless, with pesky parasites pressing his paradise, over death he quietly agonized.

He traversed the map, served Arrack and Cognac at his ritzy, glitzy flat, listened to the artistic Bobby Womack, and had the gift of gab, so he was certainly a catch, but the bachelor, Mack, didn't nap with a chick in his shack. He loved thick women with fat asses and racks wrapped in lilac, but what he didn't miss was the inevitable crap—baggage, haggling, yapping and talking smack—that caused a chapped slap to attract a gasp. So at last, the only kitty he kept in his pad was a jet-black cat called Cracker. However, he would visit an occasional kennel. With whistles and signals, he was skillful at raising and training official Pit Bulls from little, when they were blissful and only nibbled on gristle.

His activity in the infantry visibly increased his proficiency and persistency to a degree of brilliancy, which immensely benefited his illicit industry. Maturing during his enduring touring, he reaped a heap of techniques, with his feet on concrete, beaches and the backseats of jeeps. As a vibrant private, he acquired refinement from some of the wisest fighters, while his rank was steadily rising. He earned medals and learned lessons about aggression, weapons, and apprehension suppression to lessen stresses. Every now and then, from an endless list of tips, some of those lessons he expressed to his friend, Nick, to assist in countering any conflicts or risks. Some were a little fickle and simple. Others were mysterious and needed serious heeding. Following are a few for anyone who is reading:

-Light cigarettes at night and that vice might align your silhouette in the precise sniper scopes of foes' sights.

-Keep rifles with ammunition in addition to oil, but void of the stifle of grimy sand and soil.

-Just in case, it's no waste to tape on your waist a whetted bayonet.

-Watch for the threat of these Mach 3 jets. Their pace and acquisition transition are the quickest yet. They throw erosive

explosives through open windows when the cold wind blows over domes still low on pillows.

-Perpetually improve. Shoot and scoot; continue to move.

-The more you sweat in peace, the less you bleed in war. Thus, pain is weakness leaving the flesh through pores.

-Like SEALs, kneel and enact the acronym SLLS: Stop, Look, Listen, and Smell, to reveal traps, pitfalls and fails.

-To the boldest or most modest, tomorrow is not promised. So do what you must every day. Don't hesitate to spray a robust UZI or AK, just to leave fewer shooters for the rest of us to ambush, rush and crush.

Most of Mack's lessons and suggestions Nick questioned as reflections of an enraged, and possibly partially deranged, old man who spent too many days in strange lands from Sudan to Afghanistan.

What Nick came for was under the floorboards: An AK-74, a CZ-97 with four mags., a stash of flak jackets, two to three heavy-duty Israeli UZIs, two M4A1s, a scoped Remington 700 and a rope for repelling from or scaling something.

The military taught Mack many tactics and habits to grapple with sporadic clashes in battle, but his specialty was weaponry. After exchanging pleasantries, Nick didn't tell the full complexity of his destiny, only that he was readily putting his life in jeopardy with future felonies and would need to keep a few pieces of that same said weaponry.

After Nick picked through and packed a few of Mack's ratchets in a duffle bag—usually used to smuggle cash—they sat and had a chat. They rolled weed in Phillies and smoked like old chiefs greeting and holding a peace meeting in a tipi.

Mack had flashbacks nearly as often as he hit the sack. He was a victim of his own prison of visions, from missions he wished were fiction. From most, this side of himself he tried to hide, but in Nick he decided to confide.

"So you have flashbacks, in your dreams, every night?" asked Nick.

Mack released the weed smoke from his lungs and passed Nick the blunt. "Damn near."

"How do you deal with that? Live with it?" asked Nick.

Mack shrugged. "You just do, you know? But… the weed does help."

"Yeah," said Nick, thinking for a second of his own night-mares. "What are they like?"

Mack was staring at a line of trees about two hundred yards from his house. "Most are similar in some ways." He locked eyes with Nick. "I can tell you what I saw last night. It's still pretty clear."

Nick nodded. "Yeah, let me hear."

High from the lye, Mack started to describe the latest bar-barism he envisioned:

"Like lightning, gun fire striked and fighting ignited like dynamite. Blinding lights from flares glared in the air, binding the scared. Rockets left us shell-shocked. The deafening sound drowned out yells of death to breathless depths. My heart started racing, arms shaking. Forevermore, my mind is scorched and deformed by the horror of hordes of marauders, on the shores and borders of the waters of our course, pouring a torrent of torment and leaving torsos torn. I remember team members being dismembered by the torture of mortar rounds pounding the ground around our squad. My friend Jim was missin' a limb but lived. Melted metal left several men perished, some beheaded. Shotgun pellets pelted helmets, as we were enveloped with hellish, unexpected methods that tested merits, as well as vests. The smell of dead flesh festered. Our boats held grotesque shells of soldiers roasted to the molars and smoldering with grody odors.

With no proximal optical obstacles, I was lying prone behind a zeroed scope when I first opened a hole in a bloke's throat. From there, the gore of war bore a gorge in my forehead and spread dreaded images of the dead as if embedded eggs. I could see images of appendages in ditches.

Our ominous, communist adversary's military wasn't technological, but in actual battle they crept from the crevices of our premises as definite professionals. Often you needed to get 'em sleepin'. Creep behind them like real quiet mimes and *hit them in the blind. Choose a decision to kick out his mind with two from a silenced nine or slip a six-inch ice pick incision into his spine's disks.*

When it was time to strike, you had to stick-and-move quick to get missed in this multidimensional, unconventional conflict. If you couldn't run, when little missiles come flung at your lungs and loved ones from submachine guns, your middle would get critically riddled. After cutting off your tongue, fingers and thumbs, you could get strung in the sun—"

"That shit's crazy," said Nick, blowing smoke, lying back in a chair on Mack's patio.

Mack was staring into the distance like a scared hare, then he ran a hand through his hair. "Yeah. It's crazier when you're there."

"Now, those are some real gory stories of glory," said Nick.

"Well, often gory, but not much glory," said Mack. "At home, and overseas, I've seen too many men put in a hearse and beneath the dirt with worms."

"Is that how it went down when you were in the Marines?" asked Nick.

"Pretty much. But it wasn't always as bad. But in my dreams, the flashbacks are always the worst; like stitched glimpses of the abyss of perdition."

"Damn, man. I never knew that. That's fucked up. How do you deal with it?"

"You just do. Some nights I can close my eyes and sleep… in peace. Some nights I can't, ya know?"

"Strangely, I think I do," said Nick.

"Well, you get back here and nobody gives a damn about… what you did… or what you're dealing with."

"Did you leave the Marines because of the constant dreams?"

"I wouldn't say that," said Mack, "the dreams didn't start until after I got back. I left because those motherfuckas were doing everything they could to get theirs. So, I figured, I need to do everything I can to get mine. Wrong or right. Besides, they were kickin' folks out left and right at the time."

"You felt like they were just workin' you?" asked Nick. "Like exploiting you? Maybe you were putting in more work than you were actually compensated for?"

"You know, that's part of it, man," Mack replied, as he thumped the blunt's ashes at his side. "But that's something everybody has to deal with, no matter where you work. If you're not part of that top ten percent, they get a hundred dollars out of you for every dollar they pay. So there's never a fair exchange."

"And most don't even make a living wage. Enough to save. Maybe to have a baby and happily raise a family," said Nick.

"Damn, right. That shit sucks," said Mack. "But… there are two types of people in this world; those who work on command, and those who work at will."

"You think maybe they really can't afford to pay people more?" asked Nick. "You know, some companies say they'll have to fire a bunch of people if they pay any more."

"Man, please. These companies make billions in *profit*. Every year. And they hand out tens, if not hundreds, of millions in bonuses. The problem is insatiable greed. They feel the need to exceed the previous year's profits, in perpetuity. And when they don't exceed they call it a *lost*. Ain't that some bullshit? A *lost*. Because they made a profit of only ten *billion*. Mothafuckas."

"And wages…" Nick began.

"Remain the same," Mack intervened. "And that may be the most egregious slap in the face, concerning workers; the fact that profits and economic growth have gone up substantially over the last five decades but minimum wage hasn't changed. I bet you most folks are living check to check; barely staying afloat."

Nick leaned in. "Speaking of bonuses, what they should do is give *every* employee a bonus. *Somethin'*. Profit is made from everybody's labor, whether it's mental, physical, or whatever. And even if the major corporations gave all employees a living wage, they would still make huge profits."

Mack put his hands up as if trying to stop a dump truck. "Whoa, slow up, young blood. Now you are trying to make too much sense."

Nick chuckled and coughed, then switched their chatter to a more personal matter. "Hey, man, do you ever feel bad, or have any regrets, for stuff you did? I mean, this street shit since leaving the military?"

"*Man, fuck that*!" Mack hissed, deflecting and becoming defensive. "Yeah… alright… ain't nobody perfect. I know I've done some bad shit or whatever. But come on, man, they murder, maim, and displace people every day. All for the sake of corporations. Claiming it's in the name of liberation. *Man, please.* If they really wanted to liberate people, and so-called improve their quality of life, they got a whole damn continent they can get started on."

"Africa?"

"Damn, right."

"But how much can they profit from liberating, or helping to build up, a place like that?" asked Nick.

"Not much," said Mack. "But when they fly to the rescue in a place like Iraq, or Vietnam, that's precisely their pretense; they claim it's in the name of *democracy* and *liberation*. So why can't they go to Africa, and other places that are just as fucked up, and do the same damn thing? Bring those people democracy, liberty and a better life…   And personally, I honestly feel like we shouldn't get involved in other nations' affairs. But if the U.S. feels the need to wear a badge, why not do it to truly help, like serving and protecting other humans?"

"But *they* are largely responsible," said Nick, "America that is, and Europe, for the condition Africa's in today. Are they not?"

"Shit yeah, they are," the Marine agreed, sitting up in his seat. "They rushed in and colonized the place, took what they could get, and left it in shambles on their way out." Mack started waving frantically. "Byyyye! Arrivederci! Hasta luego! Fuck you! Good luck."

"But they won't go back and clean up the mess they made, because, why? It's too much work? Or because they can't see turning a profit?"

"Now, don't get me wrong," said Mack, "if they put their focus there, a profit could be made. A profit can be made damn near anywhere. But they would have to invest a hell of a lot of time and money. They would literally have to change those people's lives. Really make it into a place worth having a McDonald's on every corner. But that would require so much in resources, effort, and *willingness* to invest—and that's not something America readily does fairly."

"So, you don't see it happening?"

Mack shook his head. "Hell, no. No time soon. Why would they when they can just, for all intents and purposes, take over an oil field... or diamond mine or some shit. Besides, if they can benefit from the natural resources, they don't really need to invest in the country or the people. It's a no-brainer. Easy paper. Or at least much eas*ier*... American and European companies already make huge profits from the natural resources of third-world countries. Why give a fuck about the people? When you can leave them in penury and get away with the loot? It's easy fleecing of gold, diamonds, oil, iron, tungsten, rubber, cobalt, copper, coltan, platinum, uranium, you name it."

"Not to mention," said Nick, "the millions of people here, and I guess around the world, too, who they already exploit, and disregard, to make a profit."

"Millions? *Hundreds* of millions," said Mack. "There is nothing they won't do for profit. *Nothing.* Do some research, young blood, you'll see. *They*, banks and corporations, with the backing of a vast military industrial complex, federal agencies, policing forces, politicians and litigators, have fucked up a lot of lives. A *hell* of a lot... Not to mention how much they fucked this planet up. Petroleum, plutonium, pollution, oceans filled with plastic waste—"

"Well, what do you think about people just working hard and moving up the totem pole?" Nick proposed.

"I'm all about hard work. I *hate* lazy people. Like *sincerely* hate them. But let me tell you somethin', man. The higher you go up the socio-economic pyramid, the less room there is. It is physically impossible to squeeze more people in the top," Mack explained, then repeated, "Physically, economically, and logically, *impossible*. It really is like a pyramid, for Christ's sake! A relative few will squeeze through, but the majority will always be at the bottom. Or beneath. There can only be so many CEOs or district managers. Only so many A-list actors or pro-athletes. What they need to do is just give workers a fair share."

"Like partners," said Nick.

"Well, they are. And even if *that*—just working harder—would work for people here in the U.S., what about those all around the world who work for scraps and crumbs, as opposed to the noodles and bread they get over here? Where's the opportunity for them to work hard and move up that *totem pole*? What do you tell minors working as miners in Niger and the women locked in sweatshops in Bangkok for American and European markets' stocks?"

"I guess there's not much I *can* tell them."

"My point is," said Mack, "it's not always possible for people to just shut up, work hard and improve their lives. In some circumstances, it's nearly impossible. More so in places like Palestine, Liberia, and Honduras, but also right here in the U.S.

We're much closer to the throne, so we're much more likely to get bigger, better scraps from the table of the elite. And we're more likely to succeed. So, I guess there's a scale of struggle and indigence; and we're lucky enough to be on the lower side of that scale, but that doesn't make it any less real or pertinent."

Nick started to reply with a question, "If shit is really so bad..."

"Under this system, it is," said Mack. "I know things could be a lot worse, but they could also be a whole lot better."

"...then why don't more people say something, or do something about it?" Nick finished.

"Many reasons," said the Marine, then started to preach, "Some people feel like this is just the way it is and nothing can be done about it. Many people are pacified just well enough to keep them from doing anything. You know, welfare and shit like that. A lot of people are so distracted with a bunch of other irrelevant bullshit: T.V., games, social media..."

Nick jumped in. "Yeah, it's like everyone's head is buried in their phones and computers nowadays."

Mack nodded in agreement then continued with his sermon. "Then, you have people who are so preoccupied with their own struggles at home that it's difficult for them to really rally, rise up, revolt, or anything. Not to mention the dependence many people have on these companies. If you don't work, you don't eat. People feel like they gotta take what they can get to get by, even if it's a yearly raise of a measly dime."

"That's fucked up, man."

"Yeah, they got 'em by the balls."

"Ouch!"

"Ouch is right. So, you ask me if *I* have any regrets? Being honest, yeah, there are some things I'm not proud of. But the government *is* hypocrisy. Corporations *are* hypocrisy, when dealing with us… When dealing with the rest of the world, for that matter. You have to understand that America's foreign policy is one of hypocrisy. They try to portray themselves as some benevolent force ridding the world of evil and ushering in democracy and justice, but in reality they only do what is in their own self-interest, despite if it's wrong or right. It's a double-standard. This country has supported brutal regimes and atrocities all over the planet. So, when it comes to mine, I sleep fine. The Mafia is really no worse than these countries. Spain, England, Germany, France, the U.S., they all have a history of theft and murder. They wouldn't be the countries they are today without all the murder, theft and oppression they've benefitted from, across the globe *and* on the backs of their very own citizens. They wouldn't have as much wealth. They wouldn't have as much power and influence—leverage. And, like the mob, they too function in corruption, treachery, and nepotism. So, I say fuck 'em. Plus, you gotta remember, this is a country that parades and celebrates despicable savages the likes of Christopher Columbus. This is a country that said it was perfectly okay to shoot people, beat the shit out of 'em, burn 'em alive, or hang them from trees, without retribution, as long as they were the right color."

"I guess you're right," said Nick, "countries themselves have done some pretty bad things."

Mack shook his head heartily in agreement. "That's why you don't see many black people with American flags outside their house."

"Why do you think that is?"

"Well, have you?"

"Well, no," said Nick. "But I'm just wondering why exactly do you think that's the case. You were in the service, so what's your take?"

"Proudly," said Mack. "I was proudly in the Marines for over fourteen years. Some of the best years of my life; mostly because of the men to my left and right sides. I would've died for any of my guys. It's a camaraderie the likes of which you'd be hard pressed to experience elsewhere. Maybe sports; football, basketball, soccer, lacrosse. But even then, you're not literally putting your life on the line for your team... So, yeah, it's pretty deep. Long lasting. Forever, it stays with you."

"Yet you still don't have an American flag flying outside."

"It's different for black folks," said Mack. "Including some of us who've served. Once you're aware of everything that flag represents, it's difficult to make peace with that and beam with pride." Mack became quiet.

"What do you have in mind?" Nick asked.

"That flag is supposed to represent the so-called greatest country on earth," said Mack. "It's supposed to stand for freedom, justice, opportunity, equality, bravery, and, according to those who wear and wave it proudly, all things righteous. But the sad truth is, that is the flag under which millions of black people were marched into slavery, held in slavery, tortured for resisting slavery. Families were literally torn apart, dismantled and trampled under that flag. And don't get me wrong now, most black people are well aware of how fortunate and lucky they are to live in a country like the U.S., as it stands today. However, that does not change the fact that when people of color see the American flag they are both consciously and subconsciously aware that that very flag waved high over the bowed heads of people who suffered unimaginable agony, stress, and grief, from not only slavery but also Jim Crow, the Black Laws, convict leasing, public lynchings and deprecation. I'm talking about hundreds of years, and many, many generations."

Mack paused to gather his thoughts, then continued, "Native Americans were abused, deceived and nearly annihilated under that gold-fringed red, white and blue banner. So when I see the American flag, I think of the Trail of Tears. I think of Emmett Till. I think of Medgar Evers. I think of the Scottsboro Boys and the Central Park Five. I think of black people being beaten and spit on with sour phlegm when marching and sitting in peace, with no one being held accountable. I think of wealth inequality and disenfranchisement. That flag makes me think of mass incarceration with no intentions of rehabilitation, police brutality, and how long and hard people had to struggle for basic Human Rights and Civil Rights. And still things have not been made right. And still no one has been brought to justice. And still there has been no restitution. That flag represents taxation without actual representation, and FBI targeting of organizations fighting for justice, equality and respect. To many people, it truly is a beacon of hope. But to black folks in particular, it is a symbol of so much more."

"What about the National Anthem?" asked Nick. "Do you stand when the flag is out there?"

"Of course," said Mack. "This is still my country."

"Yeah, I hear you," said Nick. "But listen here, Mack, I have to get outta here. I really appreciate everything, man. For real."

"Youngblood, I don't know what you got planning, but I trust you. I just wanna leave you with this, 'The most powerful force on earth is the human mind. Be careful how you use it.

It's capable of making possible anything it imagines. It can solve the unsolvable. But it can also destroy you… and those around you. Or meet people's needs, heal diseases, eradicate famine and poverty—"' Mack was staring into the distance again. Like his eyes, his words were as sharp and straight as a blade. "And if you *really* wanna change the world, change yourself. Improve yourself. Educate yourself; your biggest enemy is ignorance. And don't fail to evaluate what's wrong with *you, before* you start pointing out other people's flaws and faults."

The two stood and shook hands. Nick took the tools he looked through and approved to be all-good. Then he drove to his humble abode in the hood. On the road, something had his mind hooked. Maybe because they came from a career crook, but Mack's stern words hit a nerve. *"Be careful how you use it."* A bit of introspection caused Nick to consider the rejection of his own life's current direction, a path of death, theft, and coveted aggression.

An unidentified type of bird took flight and swerved through the sky, slicing it with a wide swipe like the final dying strike of a defied samurai grinding against rising tides of rivals.

Jason's Tribulations

On the other side of the city, smothered amongst women who were stunningly pretty, Jason pondered as he wandered in a free sponsored concert in Garvey Park. Uncrowned, underground rappers from all around were there to spit freestyles that baffle, dabble in battles, and tryout ballads on the cattle-like rabble in a gaggle on grass and gravel.

A rally was underway for an array of celebrations. There was a hefty population of very animated spectators—varied by all races and ages—assimilated at two stages. Most seemed motivated and elated. Only a few were inebriated. One fought being instated as an unstable, reprobate patient. He was afraid of the results of an evaluation. As of late, he was often nauseated and easily irritated, some of his memories had faded, and he was incapable of copulation. A strained melee was taking place within his fraying brain. Jason's sense of stability and limits was missing rivets and beginning to unhinge.

Far from dark, the park was packed. The radio-hosted show was flowing into the fourth act. Most cats actually had dope rhymes over some fat tracks. Jason was listening to this eccentric kid spitting something a little different but intricate over a remixed, memorable Biggie hit:

"...the kid is arrogant and airsick/ from cosmic antics/ graphic comic and sad shit/ donned in gothic/ stickin' chopsticks/ Phillips and flat tips/ in this frantic cop chick's/ ass, tits and optics/ when she's boxed in the cockpit/ sippin' a blended, splendid/ crockpot mix of tropic/ codfish and chocolate till/ fat fills her pockets/ quick switch the topic/ or watch this with a FOX spin/ then on CNN/ still choppin' and sniffin' arsenic/ it's drastic, can't mask it/ sittin' at the brink/ of drinkin' acid/ and 26 aspirin/ skip class, crash in/ sink deep, sleep sealed beneath/ a trash lid or risk catchin'/ a kick in my ass end/ give Ben a pen stabbin'/ pass my kin cash then/ dash in plaid stitches clad with/ plastic Jackson jackets/ zipped in/ mashin' in traffic/ in a stolen cab blastin'/ elastic vō-cab at/ slow crab bastards/ no question askin'/ the MAC-10 will smash in/ the villain's cracked glass chin/ get away, escape with fake/ air-operated plates/ celebrate, bake a cake, make/ that lady Jake's wake and casket/ a classic like Janet's assets/ will I still think/ these thoughts of madness/ when the mansion I sought/ is

bought, and stock/ options cashed in/ laughin' in patches/ pitch black, trapped in/ coughin' off/ my coffin's ashes ... " As he rapidly rattled through raps, the amateur had to catch his breath. *"...when did skills stop/ in Hip Hop... not hating just stating the facts/ most of these rappers are wack."*

The shouting crowd was definitely entertained. As the kid left the stage, they gave him much praise. Jason could hear sincere skill with the ear of a rap engineer. Apart from revering the art, he was here to clear his thoughts of sheer crap and merely have a beer.

His stride was rife with the stretch of life's strife. His teeth weren't cleaned. His jeans needed to be steamed. His shirt was worse. His face was laced with a subtle stubble, but wasn't scruffy or bumpy. It was unlike Jason to look grungy, but he was bothered by an awkward thought he harbored about his lover this summer. He missed a number of suppers, so it could be she snuck undercover with one of his runners, the bumbling plumber, a buddy of her brother, or just someone younger.

About the list of deliberate, belligerent sins he committed, he was indifferent. However, before his vindictiveness and extensive ends, with women he was distant and diffident. Since his loss of riches, and subsequent imprisonment, with his wife he was now excessively possessive and protective. But unreceptive of her deceptive perspective on defective contraceptives. Hence, she was unsuccessful in her objective to fence him in with children. She became tired with his lies and decided to take a flight to Memphis in six nights. The mortified Gemini sipped Mai Tais and wine to unwind while she whined to her cousins and mother in the meantime.

Shifty and suspicious, Jason drifted in the crowd intermittently whispering a mix of contradictions, criticisms and sentences of senseless gibberish.

"In attempting affliction, rifts exist at the bridge… at the bridge… at the bridge—"

"Consists of blends of tension, suspense… Will we get fidgety, flinch? Fidgety… fidgety…"

"Elicit the assistance of an innocent friend in this incident? Innocent incident… incident… innocent…"

Anyone who sensed his spastic whisperings simply lent no attention to what was none of their business.

"Risky. Risky… She's a cheat I'm convinced. Get beat hits with fists… get beat…"

"Sick of thissss this shit. Resist sphinx afflict… afflict… afflict…" His voice trailed off as bits of lucidness suspended his madness.

Enervating ideas penetrated and dominated Jason's concentration. Strange images would breed in the breeze between the braids of his mane with migraines. He made a trip from Maine to Austin in August for an auction, and had also driven to an office in Boston without proper precaution and got exhausted.

Since then, he was convinced he often sensed violins skim the wind. It was every now and then, as if a switch is flicked to permit instruments to get in in increments. He attempted intently to pretend he didn't, but there it was again, insisting to be listened to like a two-year-old kid. Even sitting silent in his den, it would just kick in. In addition, Jason terribly needed therapy, primarily for his regularity of vulgarity, infidelity and jealousy. A lousy spouse who pounced on any ass with a bounce, he was still seething from dreaming he was seeing his wife cheating this week.

Maybe his lunacy and delusions were karma, due to him screwing Barbara, Marsha, and Carla, too. Or maybe it was karma, or voodoo, garnered from the slew of harm he used to do:

An imp who once relinquished a judicious Bishop of his trinkets, Jason didn't lend credence to grievances, pity or repentance. He once mentioned to an assistant, "This business is dependent on swiftness of shipments, not condolences for opponents or forgiveness of witless witnesses."

Well, back when the deli was readily deadly, the former informant, Jerome, wore a recorder and formed a rapport with the core of crass cats who stacked cash through the door—from a stash of crack and smack—of the corner store. Furthermore, he implored enforcers adorned in uniforms to swarm at the end of the quarter, when it was warmer, to score more dope and dough galore. The Capricorn was only a phony, but a forceful performer, who spoke of corpses and torture, and supposedly adored disorder. And he swore he drove an Explorer, loaded with coke in the floor, over the border. In short order, the thorn conformed and was adored in the orbit of the hornets on the corner.

Jason was to blame for the brazen man being taken and caged in a dank, vacant basement—ancient but insulated and painted—to be slain for making statements and being late with payments. Naked in an archaic crate, Jerome was forsaken— left to die of starvation and dehydration. He was mistaken to think that depravation was better than the hastening of a shell casing. Agents from the station never came in to save him, so the pressure of the fluorescents didn't end till day ten. Neglected, he wept and reflected on regrets under the steps. In retrospect, the wretched pest assessed his best bet would've been to deflect from transgressions and collect legit checks than to commence with offenses that ended in confessions at the behest of detectives.

Under a cultural sculpture, structured for the struggle of people of color, a cluster of young thugs turned a small scuffle into a shoving and pummeling rumble of innumerable knuckles. Teens and adults started to flee that part of the park before harmless barks became heartless sparks, leading to a meaningless stampede. It was senseless, but a consensus amongst blacks; a few awful apples making the whole batch look bad.

As if in deep concentration, Jason's eyes were squinted. "Attempting to inflict, a rift will exist…. A rift will inflict… inflict… inflictinflict…"

"Consisting of tension and suspense, will you get fidgety… flinch? Fidgety… fidgety…," whispered Jason to himself, as if he were a CD on repeat. "I think I'll cross the bridge. Cross the bridge… The bridge."

"Cross the bridge rift could exist will you get fidgety? What of dignity? Dignity… Ready for this?"

"Sick of this *thisss* shit…"

As Jason began to break away from the pack, a rude dude he knew from way back, named Jack—a Jamaican native—tapped his back. He terminated Jason's getaway simply to downgrade banter to slander and inflate an irate conversation into deprecating smack. His crabby cast of lads had him gassed—claiming he had a knack for cracking snaps, even on the handicapped. So, blowing grass and sagging with his pants past his ass, the ghastly chap passed Jason and laughed, "This fag was the ass of the class. He had no swag. His shoes and clothes looked like rags. We used to smack the naps on the back of his neck and snatch his snacks. I remember we even snapped on his mom and dad."

The brash cat harassing and throwing jabs had a bad habit— he ridiculed anyone he knew, without ever considering the conclusion.

Since age twenty-two, Jason would shoot excessively disrespectful and rude dudes, but he elected to leave instead of making a scene with the silly ninnies. It was true that as a destitute youth he didn't have three pennies, and though he was embarrassed, he had parents who didn't care if he perished in Paris at the hands of a zealous terrorist on an arid terrace.

"Rifts... What of tensions... flinchin'," muttered Jason. "What when I didn't give? Was there even one that did... really... give a shit? Tired... so fuckin' tired."

Taking a breather, he grumbled and fumbled with the keys to his Beamer. But the strain to remain a latent, graceful angel was painful and shameful as the baneful gang chuckled and mumbled all the way to his bumper.

Today, Jason was strangely at a loss for words. But not his Mossberg. With a muzzle on his befuddled tongue, and a strumming in his skull, he rummaged in the muddled trunk. What was to come was the busting of the unlucky busters' bubbles. He wanted to chuck them a shuffled puzzle to unravel in the gravel. Act as the crumbs' judge and crush them under a cudgel or gavel.

As if dumb as ducks stuck in mud, the bunch sucked on a blunt that stunk like skunk and continued to talk tough. "What the fuck you gonna do, get a gun?"

Arrogantly, they grossly underestimated his famously tenacious hatred for aggravation. He was no longer evasive. And in his present mind frame, Jason had no patience, only pangs of frustration. Brazed to the vertebrae of his nape was a pate-shaped grenade; too engaged in profane play, no one ran as they pulled the pin that began the ten-second delay—1... 2... 3... 4... 5... 6... 7... 8......

As an obscene ringing dinged into his brain, he made a brisk fling without gripping the sling. Braced at the waist, the Haitian started blazing and waving the reverberating twelve-gauge from the gang's swank laces to their faces. The blasts that rang were not bangs but bomb detonations. In his wake, he left three kids of another nation splayed and wasted adjacent to shell cases on the pavement; promulgating, heinously, without contemplation, the self-obliteration of his race.

As he opened craniums with titanium, the unstable interim stadium turned to pandemonium from the curb to the podium. Everyone was terrified as if trapped inside a twister-tossed trailer tumbling through town; their world suddenly turned upside down.

Evidently, he was stricken with some sadistic sickness. It was simplistic and uncharacteristic that he would kill anyone, even those bothersome punks, in front of mothers and kids, amongst so many witnesses. For this level of ferociousness, he needed a diagnosis. Or maybe hypnosis, if it was only a loss of control over his emotions. Either way, as if he were brain-washed with chaos at a séance, he was becoming just a sunken husk of the robust hulk he once was.

The steel was only revealed for five life-shattering seconds, but he still thought someone caught sight of the staggering weapon. Would they lie or answer questions? He might be identified for the homicides, but with the way things were go-ing in his life, he didn't really mind. However, his instinct was to run and hide. Once he shut the trunk, he jumped in his ride and headed for the upper eastside.

The perplexity of the disparity and polarity of peasantry and those of a pedigree of prosperity is a parody of hilarity.

People's Pains

Behind a blue curtain, devised for dividing persons, nurses were alerted concerning Trixy's kidneys hurting. One of the nurses, who served her lunch on trays, learned of her brush with the grave and earned her trust within days. Nurse Stacy was referred to Trixy, who deterred her from transferring. The two conversed for days and learned that adverse and perverted occurrences of their lives, as well as dreams they had at night, resonated and related in many ways. An introvert, the nurse preferred to defer and coerced her to reaffirm their assertions first.

Trixy emerged from another short hibernation drained, aching, hazy and unaware of where she lay. As the suffocating weight faded, the blurred shapes of the room interspersed then merged. Soon she could clearly see the nurse and discern her words. She was captivated when the nurse stated that meditation might facilitate her fluctuating situation more than medication.

"I know you're in pain, but be patient," said the nurse. Standing on Trixy's right side, she looked her directly in the eye. "Try to relax your mind. You're still traumatized. Besides, between you and I, some of these drugs can ruin your life."

Despite her weakness, Trixy was speaking. "I had another frightening dream last night."

In her sedated state, she navigated denigrating and eerie dreams that deeply permeated her brain. Now awakened, she craved to narrate her latest as if explaining it verbatim from pages. As she worked to confirm what occurred while immersed in the whirling dream world, her words were slightly slurred:

"I leave the latrine to see a lady on the couch. I creep closer and notice that this woman pushed me out—my mother, once much tougher, but now suffers. I shudder, at thirteen, and pray to the unseen for the umpteenth time about this routine. But would even blaspheme if it would bring me a vaccine. I believe her seemly sweep of breathing and heart beating may have been completed. Or maybe, hopefully, she only needs caffeine, three Equals and cream.

While tears rise and swirl in the frightened eyes of a girl who hasn't smiled in awhile, I reach out the unsteady, sweaty hand of a heavyhearted child. To my delight, it seems she will again see sunlight. Nevertheless, my eyes still cry wild, winding lines as wide as the Nile; for I am afraid she will not make the stretch to the day's sunset. It is only the beginning of a new day; during the rest, I expect pests to beset and dissect our unprotected nest.

There's no Cap n' Crunch in the kitchen. And a collision with crack has driven my snack and lunch into a ditch of remission. I felt imprisoned in my condition. Like it must've been some sick tradition or religion that's arisen. I try to tune, then reposition, the television with precision to envision the musicians I can only listen to, but the picture just gets thinner—it's missing an antenna.

I can see my cold toes poke from my last pair of socks. It's not fair that cash for the gas bought rocks. It's a vast mass to bear on my block; like sobbing with drops of snot in a neighbor's home, a stranger holding chrome to my mother's nose. In my throat that spot was in a knot from shock, hoping his hand didn't stammer and cause the cocked hammer to drop.

All I have is my brother allied at my side. No daddy in sight to guide me right. Sadly, we're not very tight. The only thing he's left us was broke and alone, and a debt from a loan. No messages on the phone. No presents or presence at home. No revenue. Not even a barbecue on the avenue. We have a pot, but it's dry with a white residue from diluted stew. Got a cot with spots but it's not new. And my window only shows a world with constant rain, where shots are hurled and there's nothing left to gain.

In my dream, I feel I'll be grateful the day I wake to sautéed steak, eggs and raisin bread. A glass of o.j., lemonade, or maybe grape Kool-Aid. And on the stove, four rows of rolls with a glowing coating of glaze. With all of my family embraced saying grace. In a time and place when poverty no longer plagues my race.

This dream ended like every other: Leaning at the edge of my bed, tarrying for my mother."

The nurse seemed stunned by what Trixy had summoned. "Our dreams, and experiences, are truly similar."

"Were both your parents on drugs?" asked Trixy.

"My mother," replied the nurse.

"Is she still living?"

"No. She was murdered when I was twelve. They say it was for stealing drugs."

"Oh... I'm so sorry."

"Oh, it's all right," said the nurse, her eyes lowered to the floor. "It's just that... I can recall too many memories of misery. Waking up not knowing if my mother was alive or— As I closed in I didn't know if I was approaching a corpse from overdosing or my home's core that was only dozing."

Trixy wanted to grab her hand, but the nurse was a little too far to reach. Instead, she showed empathy through speech.

"That's exactly how I felt. Too many times." She then comforted one hand with the other, wondering about her conformed mother.

"I think the crack epidemic was meant to kill black children, that's my opinion," said the nurse, suddenly feeling like sharing her philosophies and ponderings. "For which, politicians likely lacked feelings. They become numb when they can't hear us sputter blood or mutter an utter from the gutter while trying out their new putters."

"You might be right," said Trixy, "about some of 'em."

"It's like, someone far removed, flying a drone and blowing up a school. They could never do that if they had to look into the children's eyes. Likewise, it's easy to ignore the poor from a golf course."

"But do you think they're actually complicit?" asked Trixy.

"Well, just think about it. We know that the U.S. government, through the C.I.A., brought tons, literally tons, of drugs into this country. And poor, black communities suffered the greatest as a result of it. Not just in addiction, but also, and maybe worse, in being targeted in the so-called War on Drugs by the very same country that flooded your streets with those drugs. And I'm just talking about the documented and verified cases that we actually know about. God only knows how many other similar situations can be attributed to the government or government agencies."

"Yeah, that's messed up," said Trixy, "that they would do that to their own citizens."

"And then look at the crack epidemic of the '80s and '90s, which destroyed communities that were already suffering in so many ways. Addicts were treated just as badly as the dealers were, by the media, police, and politicians. Now look at the more recent opiate problems in the country, which have greatly affected rural and suburban communities. Recent addicts of opioids—pills, heroin—are treated far more like victims of disease. Trust me, they are sympathized with and sent to treatment centers. Black people were literally being kicked in the head and slapped with harsh sentences for being addicts. They were demonized. Today, there are organizations and hotlines set up to help what is now being called a 'public health problem'. Wasn't none of that back then."

"That is how it seems," said Trixy. "I've seen plenty of sad, sob stories about people overdosing on drugs. I can't remember there being any back when crack was rocking blacks. But I wanted to tell you, I like your perspective, the way you detail things."

"Oh, thank you. Well, I see this drug thing as a tree," said the nurse, then explained, "These kids on the street being beat by police are only the thin, little leaves trying to eat."

"That makes sense," said Trixy, then added, "For crumbs at that."

"If the feds, police and politicians really wanted to see the problem cease, they would uproot the tree. Cut it off at the source."

"That or legalize it and make an economic resource."

The nurse became heated. "But instead, they focus on poor people…"

"Especially poor black and brown people," Trixy offered.

"…Demonizing and further victimizing them," the nurse finished.

"Exactly," said Trixy. "And these are the people who, out of desperation, will keep taking risks, risks that are clearly irrational, to get a slice of the pie they feel they've been denied. And regardless of the crime, blacks have been more likely to do more time. Not to mention, their transition back into society has never been welcoming or accommodating."

Now irritated at the facts and ideas coming to mind, the nurse was not ready to put the matter aside. "The sad aftermath is children raising children, while the men of the village are unemployed or in prison. And children, without the necessary wisdom and experience, will bring up children with the interests and mindset of a child. All while surrounded by children and friends who don't know a thing but think they're grown before they even leave their teens. Too many parents nowadays are just kids; who prioritize a wardrobe of dope clothes, bling, thrills and entertainment over life-skills and education."

"Sounds familiar. Sounds like friends *I* had. And it is sad," said Trixy.

"Sometimes that kinda stuff is too much to think about," said the nurse. "Like today, I was thinking, 'We're at the bottom.' Jobs, pay, education, housing, business ownership, you name it; we're at the bottom."

"What do you think is the biggest reason for that? For what seems to be black people's downfall, disparity of prosperity, and destruction?"

"They reneged on Reconstruction. *They* being the government. They pathetically, and intentionally, failed black people. Always have."

"What is Reconstruction?" asked Trixy.

"Reconstruction was…," nurse Stacy hesitated, while contemplating her explanation, then attempted to make it simple and plain. "Well… after its citizens profited from the enslavement of blacks for hundreds of years, the government decided that they would help former slaves, after the Civil War, to catch up with the rest of the country. This meant getting up to speed in things like education, employment and land ownership. *That* was *supposed to be* Reconstruction. But it never happened. Not in any real sense. So those newly freed slaves, with absolutely nothing, had to do whatever they could to claw their way up a crooked and arduous social ladder. All while weeding through Jim Crow, the Black Codes, convict leasing, redlining, white flight, segregation, disenfranchisement, dehumanization, denigration and overall blatant oppression and discrimination."

"Maybe everyone discriminates, in some ways," said Trixy.

"This was racist discrimination," said the nurse, "from politicians, businesses, and everyday citizens. Discrimination in education, jobs, housing, and anything and everything else. Even when the government made strong initiatives to expand home ownership, and the middle class, blacks were deliberately excluded. On top of it all, there was mass incarceration through racial profiling in a glaringly biased and bigoted judicious system—from the cops to the courts. It's enough to make you sick."

"And pissed," said Trixy, sitting up and gripping her wrist.

"Yeah," the nurse agreed, "and pissed. But don't get me wrong, there have always been a lot of poor white people as well. But the one thing they've had over blacks, for a very long time, is opportunity. Just the opportunity to work hard, get a fair shot and possibly move up in life. Black people haven't *really* had that until relatively recently. So it's still gonna take some time to catch up. Socially, economically, politically, the generational baton of progress and success has been slow moving for blacks. We weren't even allowed to get in the race until whites were well ahead."

"Always the last ones hired and the first ones fired, for generations, over several decades," said Trixy.

"As well as getting less pay the whole way."

"So basically, people being treated like third-class citizens."

"Worse," said the nurse. "Literally less than human."

"Damn."

"Even after helping to build this country up. As well as fighting and dying for this country in every war waged, ironically, and hypocritically, in the name of freedom, justice and liberty."

"I don't think people realize how far behind we've been pushed, and then left," said Trixy. "There's a lot of ground we have to cover still. And obviously, the history does matter; this disparity didn't just come out of nowhere overnight. The history tells how it happened, how we got to this point."

"The fact is," said nurse Stacy, "for generations, opportunities, and the wealth generated from those opportunities, were concentrated mostly amongst white people. The obvious beneficiaries were their friends, families and colleagues—other white people. During those same generations, blacks were suppressed and left in the mud. That's why the average white family today has a net worth over $140,000, while the average black family is around $10,000."

"That's a huge gap," said Trixy. "And if the *average* is ten thousand, then there's *a lot* of people who don't have *shit*."

"Hell yeah," said the nurse. "And it's not because of a lack of hard work. A lot of theft, oppression, discrimination, corruption, and inequality of opportunity, played a huge part."

"Try telling *them* that," said Trixy. "They have no problem arguing that it was all earned fairly."

"Well, not all of them," said the nurse. "There are plenty of well-to-do, privileged people, white, black, and brown, who understand very well how lucky they are, and how different their lives could be had they been born elsewhere, like a poor village in Costa Rica, the Philippines, or India, or even right here at home in a poor neighborhood in New Orleans, Baltimore, or Detroit."

"You're right. But there are plenty of people who are willfully ignorant of the facts."

"That's true, too," said the nurse.

Despite the facial scrapes, nasal breaks, and painful staples near her navel, Trixy was stable. And she was no longer skittish as her stitches were removed. To avoid contamination, nurse Stacy irrigated her wounds. The nurse was an angel to the disabled, but she had her faults; ignoring every clause or protocol, she didn't see a cause to pause her talk even as she changed Trixy's gauze, knowing that anyone could waltz in from the hall.

"I sometimes wonder," said Trixy, looking skyward out the window, "what would this country be without black people?"

"What do you mean?" asked the nurse, taking a peek to see the cleanliness of the room's latrine.

"Well, I was thinking about stuff like music. Things that we all look at as being cool, fun, exciting and freeing. Black people are the source of all the pop music in this country. They're the source of jazz, blues, rock and roll, techno, R&B, hip-hop, and rap. And a lot of the culture that's come from the music as well."

"I've never considered that," said the nurse, "but it is an interesting question. What I do know is that all cultures have some good things to offer the world... And, sadly, but truthfully, some cultures *are* better than others."

"People don't like to say that, though."

"But it's true. Some are inherently more tolerant and progressively flexible."

"Oh, so, you're not just talking about music, and music culture, huh?"

"Sorry to change the subject like that," said the nurse. "But it just made me think of culture as a whole. Say what you will about America, but it *has* become a place that's far better to live in than many other countries. When you think of Muslim cultures in the Middle East and Africa, it's crazy."

"I honestly don't know much about it," said Trixy, "but the stuff I hear is pretty damn scary."

"America might have some issues," said the nurse, "but it's much better than living in Pakistan, Iran, Yemen, Saudi, Sudan, Afghanistan, or some other upside-down-inside-out-backwards-stan. Too much censorship and control. A couple of girls like us would lose half our rights, and freedoms, by just touching down in one of those godforsaken places."

"Yeah, that's some bullshit. Fuck that."

"And I second the motion."

Trixy turned her thoughts to their earlier talk. After a momentary silence, she started laughing, though not strongly, then she let the nurse in on her little joke. "Maybe they dream of us reachin' the completion of our complexion depletion."

"Word! Like Mike Jackson," said the nurse, adding a laugh of her own. "Then we'll have the complexion for connections!"

"That's funny," said Trixy, with a few more chuckles. "But seriously, what we were talking about earlier, 'trying to make it', it's just been so hard out here."

"I know what you mean. But I don't think it's impossible to 'make it,'" said nurse Stacy, using air-quotations. "I worked hard and became an RN. And I personally know several other people from the ghetto who've become successful as well. So it's not like people from there are just helpless and can't do anything without someone holding their hand and treating them like a child. But then... many people don't make it regardless of how hard they work. Just because I've done well for myself, doesn't mean I don't realize that there are real challenges to growing up in such a miserable place. People who haven't had to grow up like that wouldn't understand. Being born with so much already against you—"

"Like a poor education," said Trixy. "And then, like me, if the only thing your family history consists of is poverty, it's harder to break that deepening cycle. And that's gotta be true no matter who you are. Black, white, brown, red, yellow, it makes no difference. You find yourself born into an unlucky, depressing, hopeless environment, surrounded by poverty, what are you to do to escape?" With an inquisitive look, Trixy shrugged and put her palms up. "Once you figure that out, it's damn near too late. It's a good chance you'll grow up and be stuck at some menial, soul-crushing job... You got a poor education at school, then a poor education at home—"

"If any at all," said the nurse.

"When I was growing up, I never even saw my mother pick up a book," said Trixy. "Crazy, right? But I saw her with a gun once, when she was drunk on rum."

"Coming from the hood, trying to leave the streets and make it higher is like going through a meat grinder: A few will make it through, but most get ground up. The worst part, is when callous politicians look at the few who got through and actually have the audacity to proclaim that the current system somehow works!" exclaimed the nurse.

Trixy grinned. "Sinister Senators, huh?"

"Sinister or callous, yeah," replied the nurse.

"Or just incompetent. But I doubt it. That's just an excuse they throw around until the issue on the news is drowned out."

"What makes it worse," said the nurse, "is not having positive, successful people in your family and neighborhood to relate to. People you can look at and say, 'Wow, I can do that!'"

"And I think it's important to see people like that who actually look like you, you know?"

"Black people," the nurse clarified.

"Of course. When I could've used it most, I didn't see it," said Trixy. "Not in *my* family. Not in *my* neighborhood. The ghetto is where I was born and raised, so that was all I knew. I didn't experience much else. I didn't see much else. My family couldn't afford to take trips or go on vacation. We had no money for gymnastics, canoeing, or... *whatever*."

"Subconsciously, and maybe consciously, too, I think it affects your level of optimism," said the nurse. "And just the whole scope of your outlook. Just what's possible and available to you personally. A lot of people don't know any better than to emulate what they see and experience growing up."

"Especially at that vulnerable, gullible age," said Trixy.

"Of course. How do you think someone becomes a third-generation Klansman from Kentucky, or an aspiring thug from

Compton? Ignorance and isolation. Geographic isolation. Financial isolation. Isolation from other ideas, ideals, peoples and experiences."

"Yeah, and that all makes it that much harder to succeed," said Trixy.

There was a long silence, then the nurse offered another insight. "Some people are lazy though. You can't *give* their ass a job. Lazy and full of complaints rather than actions. You gotta get up and start somewhere."

"That's true. But some people just get tired of it—struggling. Starting at the bottom and clawing your way up, it can take a toll. Sometimes, you're simply out of energy; your cup is empty."

"Definitely. I get that," said the nurse.

"And don't get me wrong," said Trixy, "I've come to realize that some degree of struggle *is* necessary; it builds character, it makes you appreciate what you earn, it keeps you from being idle and entitled—"

"And struggles also make you appreciate the good times," added the nurse.

"What if there are never, or rarely, any good times?"

"Well, then, I guess there's not much for those people to appreciate."

"And it comes a point," said Trixy, "when struggle, excessive struggle, is not much less than mental torture. It can absolutely break you."

"Then some people start doing crazy stuff to cope, like having their grief briefly eased with codeine or morphine."

"Sadly. Just like I was saying; having a mother who was drunk or high on drugs for nine years of my life is part of the reason I wasn't raised right."

The nurse could see by Trixy's expression that the subject of her mother was a sensitive one. But she wanted to know how much Trixy would be willing to change how she had come up. "After the way you were raised, would you trade her for another mother?" asked nurse Stacy, then waited.

Trixy hesitated, then stated, "No, I wouldn't trade her for another mother... I just wish she had been a better mother."

Watching Trixy's mood suddenly worsen and become glum and depressed, the nurse turned their discussion back to black success. "We were talking about upward mobility," said the nurse, "and there's something I feel to be *pivotal* in the advancement of black people, but it is often overlooked, and rarely discussed."

Trixy turned her attention back to the nurse. "What's that?"

"This idea amongst blacks of *acting white*. I really think it's an issue, a serious issue, that's had terrible consequences."

"Stuck-up, nerdy black people, is that what you mean?" asked Trixy, with a gleaming tongue-in-teeth smile.

The nurse made it clear that she was serious. "The stereotyping, ridiculing, and discouraging, of blacks as nerdy or stuck-up, perpetuated by other blacks, to be exact. Singling out kids in school as *acting white* or not being *real*, I think it holds us all back."

"I'm sorry," said Trixy, "I didn't know you were dead serious."

"It is serious. Kids who standout risk being ostracized from the group. School can turn out to be a very lonely place. For children, that can be devastating, so most prefer to go along to get along."

"Yeah, I can see that," said Trixy. "Actually, I *saw* that. Even with kids who did well in school, there was an obvious desire to be part of the group, to not standout too much."

"And that meant *being black*?" asked the nurse, looking for clarification.

"It meant not standing out," said Trixy. "And the worst thing you could do in standing out was to appear to be acting white, or not black enough. When I think back, this is something that would definitely be frowned upon, and ridiculed, at my schools, especially in cliques of black kids. I can't put my finger on exactly where it came from, but there was undeniably this lingering pressure to *be real*, to *be black*, and to not *act white* or *act fake*. And the kids who talked proper, read extra books, and took their studies the most seriously, and excelled, were the ones who stood out as possibly *acting white* or wanting to *be white*."

"It's a cultural problem," said the nurse. "And it's absolutely damaging to black success. Like Malcolm said, 'Without education, you're not going anywhere in this world.'"

"Now that you bring it up," said Trixy, "in hindsight I can see how damaging that type of behavior can be. Honestly, I was one of those girls. Me and my friends would mock and laugh at those kids. We never outright went after them, but we were not nice at all. We assumed that the overachievers thought of themselves as better than us. Knowing what I know now, I would jettison those so-called friends in a heartbeat. I would've taken my studies more seriously and ignored what I thought was *cool... We* were the silly ones."

"You were a child. You just wanted to fit in, be accepted. It's understandable, it's human. And at the end of the day, not to make excuses for them, but the flat-out truth is that these kids lack the means to make proper judgments or decisions, which will affect the rest of their lives."

"They're immature. Adolescent," stated Trixy.

"Yes," the nurse agreed. "But it is in large part because their brains have not fully developed. Specifically, their frontal cortex."

"What's that?"

"Well… Let me think… It's the part of the brain that controls your ability to determine good and bad, set goals, plan, make decisions, understand future consequences of your decisions, predict outcomes, suppress urges that can lead to disastrous or improper outcomes, differentiate between conflicts in thoughts and ideas... There's a lot of important stuff your prefrontal cortex is responsible for."

"Wow. So, when is it fully developed?" asked Trixy.

"Not until you're twenty-five."

"Damn. That's a long time to be running around making decisions, especially potentially life-lasting ones."

"It sure is," said the nurse.

"You're making decisions, some of them *major* decisions, that you're not even fully *capable* of making!"

"Which is why a cultural change is needed," said the nurse. "Many of these kids don't know any better. If they knew better, they would do better. But it's more than just saying something to them about it. There needs to be a shift away from discouraging what is seen as *whiteness,* and being pressured to *be real* or *be black.* There needs to be a cultural shift *away* from that, and a shift towards encouraging academic success, proper grammar, civility, and interest in subject matter outside the norm. I promise you we will get much further as a people."

Hearing her become so passionate, Trixy thought the nurse could be an adequate activist or advocate. "You are absolutely right."

"Why not be the kid from the ghetto who enjoys ballet, Shakespeare, classical music, scientific studies, politics, even hiking, camping and bow hunting, things that have been considered white interests for far too long?"

"Like I said, I think you are definitely right." Trixy cleared her throat. "A change in thinking, amongst many people in the black community, could be a huge step in sending blacks soaring."

"Ultimately, as far as we're *all* concerned, what we really need is unity. U-N-I-T-Y," said the nurse, thinking of a Queen Latifah verse. Unity, compassion, and peace. Or at least as peaceful as can be. I wish people could see past their petty, minor differences."

"Like race, ethnicity, religion, politics?"

"Precisely," said the nurse. "See past all that silly crap and realize that we all need each other if we're going to survive in a world worth living in. That's the good thing about coming together during calamity; it enhances the sanity of humanity."

"There really are much more pressing issues for us to be concerned with," said Trixy.

"We all wanna live healthy lives," said the nurse, "get a good education, and not be incumbered with the excessive stress of simply paying bills and getting a decent meal. We all want to feel safe, without threats of assault, theft, rape, or murder. We all want to be treated fairly and with respect."

"Exactly."

"We humans fight and hate each other over the dumbest things… Politics is one of 'em."

"Which is crazy to me," said Trixy, shaking her head slightly, showing her confusion.

"Both the left and right, Democrats and Republicans, have some dumb ideas and say some dumb stuff. They both have ulterior motives and tell lies. They are both heavily subjective and biased, living in an echo-chamber of bias-reinforcement. And they all have primary objectives of getting reelected and lining their pockets."

"Word."

"But both sides, liberals and conservatives, also have some good ideas, and motives. And they are also both necessary in moving this country forward while also keeping us all safe. Or as safe as can be."

"Yeah, I guess. I just wish they were all more obsessed with doing what's best... for the people. Most people, not just cronies and companies."

The nurse noticed the time on her phone. "Whoa, time is flying! I gotta make my rounds. I'll be back to check on you in a minute. You need anything right now?"

"I think I'm okay," said Trixy. "If you can, just stop by before you leave. Please?"

"Don't worry, I'll see you. I *know* you know there's a lot of lazy nurses up in here," said the nurse, making a face.

Trixy's only response was a grin and nod, but she appreciated the care and patience nurse Stacy had for her patients.

Time is lined with archives of life's alliances in its strive to survive. Even blind vines intertwine and climb inclines of shrines while trying to find the sky to thrive.

Brother from Another Mother

"I hate people… They're all fuckin' idiots."

"That or inconsiderate."

"I'm tired of this shit. Do I even wanna live?"

"You got no kids. Just get it over with."

"Isn't that an unforgivable sin?"

"Isn't sin relative?"

Though a meeting between two beings was in full swing, no one was before him, beside, nor behind. Long before his crimes in the park, his mind started to unwind and fall apart—back when harsh girls hurt his pride and hard times sent him to the dark side. Despite the plight or onus, Jason was no longer focused. He was mentally split like a million locusts.

When Nick located Jason, he was flanking a racing track, pacing and impatiently waiting. His braids shaved to a fade and his jaded face engaged in opaque shades, he was talking while walking. Nick wasn't near, so he couldn't hear him clearly. The only other person there was a girl in thick mascara eating sticks of mozzarella and reading a novella about capoeira, starring girls named Sarah and Gabriella, under a sun umbrella.

Since an inmate, Jason's innate traits hadn't changed. A straight operator who hated vague charades, didn't tolerate irritating fakes and lames, and always separated pay from play.

On the phone they spoke briefly only to agree to a discreet meeting place. Now, face to face, they both exchanged respects, then perspectives on their respective predicaments.

It had been seven bitter winters since they met in prison, while serving sentences for similar offenses. Over fifty percent of Nick's time was spent silent in involuntary solitary confinement. At the time, he didn't realize it was a vital requirement for his heightened enlightenment—getting his mind bent and widened around the world he was dying in. This was back when he was closed in from the cold wind but his mind was unfolded and opened to old penned prose and poems of Poe and other poets—from the stoic Michelangelo to the heroic Mya Angelou. For untold minutes, he would sit pensive with a pencil, or alternative utensil, finally attentive to his own opinions, perspectives and potential.

He didn't want to return to prison, but he couldn't see himself simply working for a diminishing pension. He had a penchant for business so he thought he could go independent, if only something legit caught his interest.

After his isolation for insubordination, Nick couldn't wait to taste the paved road that raced from the main gate. When his release date came, he literally placed his lips on the gray clay bricks.

Within the gates of the state prison, lifting plates of weight with repetition, he and Jason became acquainted over quaint conversations. Their irrefutable mutual admiration was more than an unusual aberration. Conveying reputations, they shaped and framed a great relationship. Jason appreciated that Nick wasn't talkative, or timid—he exhibited confidence, but didn't impinge upon Jason's reinvented impending business for the cement trenches, once his stint in prison ended, which was significant since he struggled, from his crust to his crux, with the flux of trust and love and such.

As a preteen, Jason was kind, quiet, sweet and meek, but eventually increasingly revealed his mean streak till it equaled a peeved wolverine's. By fifteen he ran the streets, but wasn't yet unequivocal to some despicable criminal shipping corruptible chemicals. He angered educators, neighbors and strangers, and smoked flavors—no coke, only green and nicotine—but there were no indicators of major danger to the chambers of legislature.

Then, still a youngster, he was flustered and suffered for a juncture. His big brother was outnumbered by gunners he trusted—vultures who vied for clientele and sells from his already slim slice of the drug scales. While he slumbered, he was smothered under a cover, the color of blood on butter—because of a couple slugs plugged in his lungs, from which he wouldn't recover. Wrapped in a rug, he was dumped in a cluttered truck of rubber, lumber and other junk in midsummer.

Jason couldn't adjust. His conduct was disruptive for months. And all of a sudden, all he wanted was bucks, blunts and troublesome fun. He became rude, cruel and moody, and soon was in juvie.

He and his roomie, a screwy newbie named Rudy, made mad cash, and split sushi, with the staff on duty, passing pills and hits of acid to kids who were kooky and gloomy. The aftermath was a path of wrath on behalf of a passion to have more stacks and flash to brag about swag with stag scallywags.

R udy grew from juvie and the group homes and began to move his own dope. The contentious kid became a re-

lentless menace. Incredibly, he found, unexpectedly, the reci-
pes for ecstasy and methamphetamine, and steadily increased
their intensity. Immediately, riches, dope and schemes became
his wishes, hopes and dreams. Embracing the road he chose,
Rudy's goal was untold sums of rubies and gold.

As an adolescent in Texas, he was restless and ran with re-
bellious fellas destined to be felons—selling antidepressants
and other medicines of convalescents. To his parents, sheriffs
alleged he was helpless; reckless, sexist, and had a death wish.
He didn't hold life as precious, the type to kill or die for his
necklace.

The nefarious Aquarius even thought it was hilarious to get
a Mexican humanitarian, Marilyn, and a Bulgarian librarian,
Carolyn, hooked on heroin at the Sheraton. He was an outright
barbarian.

Sadly, he napped and got clapped in his snapback cap.
Never even heard the click-clack of the gat. Deep in his seat
like Poseidon in the sea, the tyrant was sitting silent chewing
Trident in his new blue Chrysler aligned beside a hydrant. He
was on assignment to grab cash for bags he gave on consignment. He was waiting for two cats who claimed to have hit a
snag, though they owed him ten stacks. However, that could've
been an innocent coincidence and mishap. His murder may
have been payback for a chick he gagged and kidnapped, or a

fiend he beat with bricks and bats. It's a fact, everybody has family, even dicks and brats.

Narcs parked in an unmarked car saw the outlaw's fall. After a thousand assaults, they didn't care who was at fault. They didn't even scoff or cough. They put salt and sauce on the take-out steaks they ate on stakeout and just drove off.

If only he listened when it was foretold that the grandiose, but morose, road he chose would inevitably lead to woes, his homies and desperados—from Colorado to Chicago—would not be throwing roses in his final resting hole before he was blessed enough to get old and outgrow his corrosive bravado.

Jason developed a strut that divulged he hung with thugs and was accustomed to fisticuffs. Soon the Haitian was racing to the tomb to the tune of a crew of screw-faced goons. They were causing unusual problems, like ghouls and goblins in Gotham. They came from the forgotten bottom, so they felt that gave them the right to play God and Robin. His incensed insistence on instant riches as essential was then indispensable from his existence in viscous mischief.

When he met Nick, he sensed a fulfilling friend the fitting equivalent of his missing sibling, in which he could infinitely depend. One who didn't pretend, and would defend his dividends in the event he was apprehended again.

They became thicker than blood in mud. Other crews labeled the two "The Bud Brothers." Before Nick was reincarcerated for unrelated, fallacious allegations, their cake came in crates like freight. But incompetent characters in his camp made copping cultivated cannabis complicated. Without a trace of cocaine confiscated from his frame, it still didn't take the Jakes long to breakup Jason's remaining organization and have him arraigned and abated to slow, patient paper chasing. All due to the dishonorable intentions of snitching stoolpigeons—giving cops a slew of clues for a slap on the wrist in lieu of their petitioned split of his revenue.

One of Nick's niches was sniffing out snitches. He tried to advise Jason but he wouldn't listen.

A t the end of a bent and upended fence, sitting on a bench and sipping a Mistic to quench his thirst, Nick first explained the gist of his quick renegade escapade for pay, then promised Jason a split if he assisted in a hit on the narcissistic cyst called Slick.

As for friends, the two were the truest. Tactfully talking tactics, together they thought things through to a common conclusion—the pimp's execution. Jason would then make a break for Bermuda via Houston amidst the confusion.

Nick explained his basic plan of retaliation to venerate the patient he awakened. Jason was willing and committed to killing the lunatic who inflicted a whipping on his friend's only sibling. Knowing that small errors could land them in the hands of pallbearers, his thinking was simply, "Better measure whether weathering the vendetta is worth the treasure." However, Nick's livid wish to clinch this frigid dish of revenge was bigger than the price of pride or riches; it wouldn't make a difference to calmly consider the consequences.

Nails would impale both wood and marrow of narrow bones belonging to righteousness in a scarecrow's pose. The priceless sacrifice is then placed on a throne—mightier than the empire he roamed. This came as no surprise. He recognized his demise was nigh while he dined with his disciples by his side. One took a bribe as a spy and left him out to dry.

Jane Saved

ince the day Jane strolled along the curve of the curb, she had been serving the Lord and learning His Word. Learning that He was both personal and merciful. Based on what she was reading, through her belief she was redeemed. The vivid introspective she gained gave her spirit continuous stimulus. With a meticulous syllabus, on the Bible she put restless emphasis. As a gentle gentile, she was attentive to the text's preciousness. And saw relevance in both Testaments, to include the recklessness of the venomous nemesis in Genesis. From what she read in Exodus, the helplessness under the villainous Pharaoh's aggressiveness led to selflessness, then cleverness. At the perilous precipice, Pharaoh was pelted with pestilence, evidence of the excellence of the Most Beneficent. In the bitterness of the wilderness in Leviticus, dissidents and their descendants, without the patience to witness the Lord's magnificence, were reduced to frivolous iniquitousness with indigenous men not fit to be His children.

Jane offered her heart to the Father to alter her life at the altar. Her main aspirations were the cultivation of her own salvation and upholding obligations and rituals with her new spiritual home. Besides sleep, her week was hugely ruled by group meetings in the cathedral with congenial people. Everyone was peaceful and heedful beneath the regal medieval steeple. Anywhere, where evil and being deceitful are treated as illegal, and everyone feels equal, there is always little upheaval.

Now that God was her parachute, she no longer flocked with prostitutes. She resolutely unglued her goofy and unruly troop from her life, and was sowing seeds to be known and seen in an improved light. She no longer felt like a helpless marionette bereft of the self-respect she was expected to shed, and that in itself was refreshing, yet blessings came as she changed her behavior from catering to tailored players to praying in faith to her savior, the maker of nature and eraser of danger. He whose dressing and resting chamber was once a nesting manger.

Not long ago, tobacco smoke billowed as she strode like an echo in the shadows of shallow and callow whores who wore yellow, retro stilettos to the gallows of the ghetto. Without question, she was the exception; the reflection of most resembled moldy marshmallows or mowed Velcro afros over mugs with moles and holes as black as crows on coal. But her sorrow was as heavy as those she followed, swallowed by the hollow of hotel doorways to be compensated a petty levy for foreplay, for a bevy of emotions flowed as her levee gave way under yet another fellow's portly frame.

No longer promenading or placed on display, today her ways had swayed. When saintly ladies arranged a bake sale, she was at the table taking orders, pouring over cake details, and bagging pastries from the weight scale. Moreover, every word of her verses was heard through the pews as if from a flute acutely tuned for soothing, therapeutic music. Only a cruel liar would dare declare she didn't woo the choir. While viewing an unusually beautiful funeral, the church stirred as they were immersed in the words of a dark dirge bursting from a heart—partly harp—buried within the belly of a cursed bird—birthed submerged in a world of fervent hurt and burden, who emerged determined to worship the Lord of the universe as bad turned to worse.

Once an apathetic skeptic, Rev. Johnny R. Rich, her prophetic cleric, was now a respected and connected man of angelic merit. As a millionaire, his wears had a rare flair, but he was filled with resiliency and had the ability to skillfully give a ministry on the trinity, chivalry, antiquity or divinity equally with fluidity. The minister's parishioners often brought visitors to listen to his signature services of purpose and sternness. So every Sunday new faces sprouted around the crowd. However, nearly every evening, the Reverend was there to change people's paths and habits, not just on the Sabbath. Every day, with prayer, praise, fasting and faith, in the church he was at work purging disturbing perversions concerning churchmen deserting and reverting to urban lurking. He asserted his version of sermons to convert persons, on the verge of burning, to serve as determined, coercing herdsmen for he who was birthed of a virgin.

When he preached, he pleaded with the people, especially the weak and fatigued. "For your soul's sake, seal the deal with the Lord—your shield, and he'll heal heels that have endured hills, valleys, pills, and the chills of back alleys..."

With a deep, riveting delivery, he continued to speak about the mystique of God and seeking to be counted among the meek. At the perfect moment, he would motion for the devotion and atonement of the chosen. "Sisters and brothers, *this* is the ultimate prize. Change your lives. As you sing hymns to Him, repent for sins and lies. Be baptized before your demise, for no one knows when it will be his or her time to die. Death comes as a thief in the night. At that hour, will you be right with Christ?"

He thrived on trying with all his might to save sinners in a city where the appetite for crime was rife and rising. By his assessment, if a pleasant peasant from the past settled in the present, the incessant sound of sirens in the city would frighten him into an asylum in seconds.

***

Invited by longtime parishioners, Jane and similarly new members were chipper at dinner with the minister. Getting fatter with laughter, they chatted over platters with manners of grandeur as if they were in their own pastor's manor. From simple sandwiches to delicious dishes of fish and chips with shrimp, they chewed food and sipped soup from spoons.

Hiding behind a menu, two booths away someone was eyeing Jane. The customer was such a glutton that buttons couldn't cover his stomach as he munched on muffins and mutton.

Other than hunger, they were at supper to discover who amongst the younger sisters and brothers were new deacons and ushers. Part of the relevant requisite was to be elegant and benevolent yet delicate and have excellent etiquette. It was also suggested to remain celibate during development.

Once the meals chilled and bellies were filled, all were paying bills, claiming coats, or saying adios. Although politely and quietly, Jane intervened with a plea as Deacon Jean was speaking to a few attendees of the feast while leaving. She was eager to catch a ride to her street this evening. He agreed and said to meet him at his money-green Jeep Cherokee.

She no longer wore short skirts, so you couldn't see her legs, but to watch her walk by still hurt a man's heads. As she did as he said, a sweat of regret was felt on his neck.

In many regions, Deacon Jean was a beaming beacon for mentally beaten men depleted to heathens. The type of men who needed freedom from legions of breeding demons feeding on their weaknesses. Teaching cohesion, and reaching to seize the peace of Eden before Eve had eaten a piece of the tree of good and evil, was deemed to be the chieftain's key reason for seeking the completion of these freed men. His sole mission was their souls' ascension. He held hopes of one day himself being a Bishop.

***

Snug in his truck, they jumped on the express and headed for her requested address. The compelling passenger, smelling of lavender, unclasped her belt fastener. She knew he had no spouse, so before they reached her house she tweaked her blouse. Layers were peeled to reveal a rousing scene that bounced. To not see her cleavage now, his eyes would have to be gouged out. She was steaming down deep in her physique to bring intriguing meat to meet the sweet, secreting stream in her petite G-string.

Jane could be seen weeping and singing songs amongst throngs speaking in tongues like she belonged, but her weakness of lust was strong. She tried to be refined. And was directly reminded of nights pulling stunts and strutting amongst bunches of corrupted sluts while discussing their crummy luck and lack of funds. But even after five months with near nuns, her fussy lust she couldn't fight and rise above in triumph.

With enticing eyes, she pleaded with Deacon Jean to feel the heat between the cheeks of her seat, but there was no need. Unexpectedly, he confessed to his bursting thirst for her flesh. His quest to undress and caress her breast with finesse was present at church as well as when he was at rest. He professed that he was obsessed with her every breath, to the onset of stress.

Jane's shape and face made him contemplate a racy lady he once dated, and impregnated. But he became frustrated, skated away, and didn't feel obligated to marriage after her miscarriage. Though relatively young, she wasn't mistaken for an unscathed vivacious grape, but she was still an amazing, radiating raisin, dainty and unappreciated, named Grace.

***

A thriller of a licker, his whiskers lingered within the sinner's slender gender as her tender center simmered and surrendered. Jane clinched her soft sateen sheets as her figure shivered like withering thinner in winter. The moist noise made her loins rejoice with vigor. And she trembled as he nibbled at the dimples near her nimble middle. It's hard to imagine the magic they made on her mattress. The two were like matches on fabric fashioned from static. It was an unsettling pleasure, like blessing the devil with peppers that burn forever.

Anointed and appointed for being poignant, he became a disappointment for a few moistened moments of enjoyment. During church appearances, she envisioned being as disciplined and diligent in the religion as he. Now this intimate incident had renewed their sinfulness.

Provoking stronger strokes of her Jonah-soaked keyhole, she rode and stroked his ego, cloaked and alone. Though they hid in her home, they were also as out in the open as being exposed to God's wrath while floating in the ocean with no more than a raft, for all things He noticed as if in a photograph.

Treason is the reason Jesus was grieving and bleeding from a beating. Likewise, it could be said that they stabbed their dapper pastor in the back with a dagger. For this matter, they would have to answer to their Master at the rapture, or the next chapter—the hereafter.

From warrants to warnings, chains to champagne and tuxedos in casinos. Reduced to ruins, he still grew with no excuses.

Kingpin

From infancy, communal deficiencies and vivid imagery of hostility instantly contributed to his present delinquency of infamy. Maybe not since a seed, but surely since being released, in his vicinity, and distantly, he was viciously the epitome of a litany of evil deeds.

The infamous pimp, Slick Rick, was born Martin Simmons. From the cradle, he was near the tables—from craps to pool to Blackjack. When he was able, he became playful for bankrolls and stacks.

Like many kids without chips for kicks, Martin was starving to get a meal in his ribs, but wasn't yet willing to steal or kill with zeal. Unlike his allies, his galvanizing ties with crime didn't derive from rebelling from his parents dwelling and declaring he was selling nickels and dimes, with pistols and knives, because he was deprived and lived a dismal fiscal life. Rather, he fingered and lingered over a cue, then figured he'd put his skills as a billiards wizard to use. As he observed his picture in the mirror, he remembered being schooled on the rules and clues to pool by his uncle Richard—a trickster who often whispered because his ticker was withered and injured from being filled with a mixture of distilled liquor and a need to bicker, principally in the midst of Bid Whist.

Soon, to his amusement, Martin was truly confusing and abusing men twenty-two years above his youth, who, after losing, were accusing him of using illusions. Some called a truce halfway through a game, then refused to pay the prudent student, due to his age.

While outsmarting marks in the dark—where men were marred with scars and bizarre women wore leopard leotards and scarves— his sharp talents balanced to include an aptitude for knowing the precise odds of dice and cards by heart. Before long, the starved nonstarters wanted him barred from all pool halls and parks. One claimed he'd make gelatin of Martin's skeleton, or at least leave it in shards, if he even played darts.

Canvassing the gambling scenes in the streets, he was establishing a serious streak, managing to dismantle anyone scrambling to challenge his elite seat. During his endeavors, he was often in spots with betters, debtors, and old storytellers, as well as peddlers of dope, but never smoked nor sold. So cats who bought a load of coke often sought to talk to him for a loan. Since they trusted his luck, through him purveyors wagered on Lakers, Blazers and Pacers. And anyone pulling a caper had faith he could flip their paper. As an unhampered rambler, the gambler was as ferocious as a Taser and as focused as a laser.

An unfortunate moment in Trenton slowed his momentum, and then some, since in his denim was an immense sum. Cops who had been watching with binoculars and monitors popped up in a popular spot in the hood looking to put their hooks in crooks known by common monikers. That fateful day, he was at a table getting paid. When the screaming police breached the threshold, the youngster flung his pole, abruptly rolled like a mole and ducked in a cubbyhole. Cops on the hunt with a hunch plucked him out of the nook. As he stood, he cussed and fussed about being booked, so he was punched and pushed. He was cuffed and stuffed in a wagon with the maddened and corrupt before he could clearly construct what had happened. He was taken and caged based on fake accusations of slanging cocaine, though he was only playing pool and poker with brokers and mediocre chokers below a kosher grocer after closing. But roaming among the paws and hooves of wolves and bulls denotes he's just as law-opposing as those droves of oafs and parolees.

From prison, a simple epistle petitioning for clemency from the conviction was written. But the decision from the reticent system insisted he finish his sentence in his inauspicious position. In discomfort, he hunkered down in the dungeon for a few dozen months, and grew accustom to disruptions erupting and becoming bludgeonings just because of someone's assumptions.

He felt fury—for the jury and the prosecutor—for being accused without proof, and that was inexcusable. His innocence fueled his virulence and lit a fuse of truculence. "If they wanna paint me as a pusher, then they'll regret it when they get the biggest pusher yet," were the words he unremittingly repeated, between rereading mail, as he sat in his teeny cell.

It was evident that he was eloquent, and as intelligent as an elephant. But his unjust punishment was a significant stimulant for his subsequent rigidness and temperament. Upon being unleashed from the beast, he was like a yearning machete emerging from its sheath. Anticipating the day, he became keen and greedy, so he hit the seedy streets to earn cheese the easiest way he had learned since a teen. Only now his fear of appearing weak often led to extremes. Eventually, he was more capricious and vicious than vipers. Seen in the streets as a snake of Satan or vampires.

From one hedged bet to the next, he collected assets. To their disparity, he impressed some of the best, and most respected, speculators with his resurrected and perfected dexterity. Before long, he baked enough bread to be a threat and then paid his own way into the dope trade.

Once he had the total of loyal personnel, an old motel as his citadel, and a strong clientele, the ignoble mogul was compelled to sell for the local cartel. With that decision, he and his minions held dominion over two of the city's bridges. That led to a minimum commitment of several shipments with Dominicans in order to avoid a cataclysmic collision.

He then had the bright idea to accrue loot by recruiting persecuted and prosecuted prostitutes—troops he would use to lure major users and entrepreneurs. As he fermented in the pen, a pimp named Rick convinced him that there were three approaches to controlling these promiscuous women, and he had the wherewithal to use them all—mental, physical and chemical—until the women were enthralled and had nowhere to fall but in his maw and mauling paws. They were the beautiful butterflies bound by the paper of walls—men whose aggression was their prison and protection.

Within weeks, six whores were reporting to get their particular fix while sending him useful tricks who were affluent and rich.

In time, his guidance, and well-defined crime alliances, gave him a license for defiance of even detectives' directives. It could've been circumvented, or completely prevented, when he still rippled with innocence. But his life experiences since an infant turned him into a repeater of misdemeanors, and a deceiver of teamsters, leaders with meager demeanors and anyone weaker—geezers, teachers, even believers on Easter.

Thunder growled as Lightning's claws crawled across the clouds. Lightning scrawled with his paw as Thunder fought to howl. An ongoing bout to announce to the denounced and devout alike what was about to abound after a drought.

Reciprocity

lad in dust masks and hunters' gloves, the Bud Brothers had half a ton of guns slung—some of the ratchets Nick plucked from under Mack's rug for the scrum that was to come. The pair was well aware of a nearing atmosphere of severe despair but sincerely didn't fear the heart-baring affair. Theirs was an air of debonair as they made for the stairs.

After a rare prayer, to spare their heirs, they dared to appear from the rear. There they could sneak in secretly and, conceivably, easily tear through the players' hair speedily like slayers' fierce spears piercing bleary-sphered deer.

Keeping their magnified sights high and both eyes wide, they climbed the height of two flights. Slick's guards were unprepared for the snare. The maggots were distracted with a tablet, chilling in chairs at the top of the stairs playing solitaire in their dough-for-blow trading lair. The scumbag's backers were drafters of disaster, gun clappers like master drum tappers, but also dumb slackers. So it was simple to catch them as they giggled and twiddled with symbols on the Kindle.

Jason put a pistol to a pimple on the senior simpleton's temple. The sentinel swiftly became sensible and didn't quibble. His chiseled image fizzled; he trembled and sniffled as snot trickled and spittle dribbled. They pleaded for reprieve, but Jason was feeling extremely steely. When the slide glided twice in a trice and retired, their lives expired with a blinding fire.

After Jason sparked the guards, they explored the floor's main corridor. Within forty yards, they regarded a door to a room used for seminars ajar. Inside was a stark blend of cigar scents from the bartering sharks and oligarchs. With the art of surprise on their side, they could smartly barge in, charge and bombard the bargaining czars.

The occupiers, lined in the finest attire, were pariahs with priors—suppliers and buyers conspiring to acquire the entire district's drug empire. They diametrically opposed and loathed messiahs and pious friars. These were callous men of malice who casually practiced madness.

Nick gave Jason a gesture to use intersecting vectors. They planned to use the terror of intrepid pressure to pepper the shelter's dwellers, whether testers, sellers, investors, or collectors of treasure from kilograms, to overwhelm and slam the clans into a realm of rams and pentagrams.

The aggressors' muzzles were muffled with suppressors. In jungle boots, the two gentlemen, imbued with adrenaline, swooped through the fatal-funnel without a stumble. Within the twitch of an eyelid, strident violence rivaling a riot was incited. The uninvited pirates blindsided and collided with the private party of the criminal minded. When they blasted clappers, glass shattered, and men of stature scattered to bypass being captured and splattered in a massacre by the attackers' staggering calibers. However, from the challengers' apertures, patterns of brain matter were still seen spattered on banisters as if by ravenous scavengers.

The unfriendly assembly of twenty was in frenzy. Instantly, they saw five wise guys fall as holes the size of golf balls opened and dissolved drywall. Some lay sprawled, others crawled and squalled, appalled that someone had the gall to befall and assault them all.

Red dots spread dread in the spot as the lead-embedded dead dropped from headshots. Those who bled and fled might've died instead from leg clots. The credulous sellers felt misled and locked in a threaded web, but traded fire at a dire range in the unexpected hotbox. But with the precision of a physician, Nick and his friend's munitions sent crimson incisions into all opposition on the premises—piggish henchmen and their insidious assistants.

Half the mustached scumbags must have collapsed in the bloodbath when there was a flashing lapse in action—Nick had finished his first clip. Enveloped in peril, he kept his beveled barrel level, and didn't use a moment to focus on the bolt sticking open. He quickly gripped a new clip filled to the tip, slipped it in, listened for the click of a perfect fit, hit the bolt release and proceeded to squeeze. Chopped down some of the mob's top men but did not stop popping.

Jason shooting the UZI loosely not only induced wounds but produced plumes of smoke and fumes as strong as the stool of goats—as he sliced through the colluding striped suits, his eyes were suffused with a ripe brume.

Amidst the pall and pitfall of the onslaught, Slick didn't stall. Breaking away like a small jackrabbit on Adderall, he dashed and hauled ass down the hall past stacks of bad mattresses and black trash baskets, as his Frïs-filled flask fell from his jacket. Nick spotted the bastard and was glad that at last he would put him on his back. As Slick escaped the volley and raced from his posse, Nick promptly moved smooth-but-fast through a path of the goons he had clapped.

After they were assailed by gales from hell, all that was left in the room was a stale smell from the pale, frail frames of decaying males draped over tables and rails. No one was left to tell the tale. They were decimated by the unrestrained rage of a hastily deranged infiltrator, on this date of fate to venerate a berated lady—who wasn't chaste or a saint, but could relate to his unabated pains as well as his mate.

The charge left Nick's arm scarred but he was hardly jarred. Blasting at his body, he tracked Slick to the shoddy lobby, headed for his wasabi-green Maserati. Twelve shells ejected in Nick's attempt to inject projectiles to intercept and infect Slick's chest and wrest from his essence a reveled conquest. Four hit the pimp's protective vest, which was enough to put him on the floor and give Nick a rest.

Since seeing his sister beaten and fatigued, Nick reckoned he was destined to threaten the street legend's regime. And at present, with one last lesson in Nick's Smith & Wesson, Slick's chess set was in check—Nick took his rook, and the rest, underfoot. Now the crooked hooker-butcher looked up at the hooded hunter hunkered above and mumbled like a crumbled hoodlum humbled at the foot of a wooden pulpit. He didn't feel the bullet when Nick pulled his index in reflex and ended his era of terror and bullshit. No time was wasted explaining the pimp's fatal mistake. With a checkmate that replaced headaches with deadweight, Nick blew away his custom Gucci frames—made for the Sun's UV rays but not a gun's pointblank blaze.

Proven to be just another deluded human, from a summit of ruling he plummeted to ruin. When he began his criminal career, Slick never believed he would be seen feeble and defeated like King Stephen of England. But with the murderous speed of a cheetah, Nick deleted the Libra-born leader, succeeding in bringing the woman-beating beast to the concrete beneath his feet. Immediately, he went from mentally empty to thinking, with a symphony of sympathy, "Maybe now Trixy can simply breathe easily, count sheep and get a peaceful sleep."

What he felt could not be expressed through language, but he knew she would languish, deflated, in a banquet of indignation and anguish until the pimp was vanquished.

***

The wheels squealed and screeched like excited swine as they pealed-out and careened down the street. As they fled, they kept the headlights low and sped through two red lights. It was the dead of night, but Nick slowed and turned on the lights as Jason reminded him that they were holding stolen kilos—blow they hoped to unload for a low price.

Two seconds sooner, Troopers in a cruiser would've viewed the shooters' maneuvers. Fortuitously, they were pursuing an eluding intruder on a scooter who was accused of boosting computers and carrying a Ruger.

After the hit, and sabotage of the entourages' deals with a barrage of steel, the two switched cars in a parking garage. Nick drove his friend to the crib, then made his way to his own home, blessed he had lived and ready to kiss his kids.

Fragmented families saddened by attachments to flattened and aban-doned pasts. Places where, when inhabited, glad granddads, talented grads and bandits with magnums had adapted to challenges and refused to lose enthusiasm. Places like Gary, where faces that carry the weight of their in-furiating fate look scary.

The Coldest Dish

I t was a minute within midnight when bristling wind whipped and snapped twigs back and whistled crisply into brick chimney stacks. Flimsy leaves and pieces of debris were tossed across the dimly lit street into wilting weeds. Then the sudden combustion of gunpowder drowned out the howl of a hound. What followed the supersonic crack sound of the round was sure to arouse future topics, gossip and chats around town.

Nick once believed, and even preached, that freedom was the distinct feel of a tree. Or at least knowing it was within reach. When he was sealed in the clink, seeing leaves swing and hearing the wind sing beneath wings, the serene scene through the steel-screened sills sent shrill screams and tears dropping from the top tier. Now he's slumped under the trunk of a tree, wheezing in the freezing breeze as his breathing increasingly flees and his heart's beating queerly creeps to a cease. Eerily, he didn't get an epiphany until "Tiffany" was the last thing passing through his teeth.

He was bucked by a chump he once struck and roughed-up at lunch—back when he was a young lunk dumb enough to put up a front and punk schmucks without guts just to get his name up amongst other flunking youngsters coming up the rungs in the game of drugs. Now that same chump was a drunken klutz with a guts-mustering gun tucked, plus he puffed plump blunts cut with a touch of angel dust. When Nick pulled up, the creep was seated between a dull, rusty muffler and a dumpster—that doubled as a temporary bunker. Matte black, his gat lacked luster. Assuming he was another junky customer, and not someone daring to ensnare and tear him asunder, was Nick's blunder. As will eventually come to all of us, life's expunging pendulum swung with a gentle hum and crushed his run of luck.

His Mrs., and kids too, will soon miss Nick. Due to ancient, but flagrant, mischief he rued, there would be no more missives, goofy Christmases on the roof, or traditions of tooth substitutions for his youths. And no vision of legit businesses from which to choose. Only emotions and mental images of tension when they reminisce and muse. He wasn't sinless, but he deserved forgiveness too.

For some, love comes and goes with the regularity of rainbows. For Nicole this won't be so. The only mate she had ever known met his fate and no one could take his place or compensate. Together, their hearts' wrote a jovial tome that evoked hope. When she was told he croaked she believed it was a hoax or an inapropos tope. As reality encroached and gave her a jolt, she almost choked as time slowed and throes crescendoed. She mostly moped, but phoned her devoted folks, the ones who scolded her when she eloped, to console her corroded soul, but they had no antidote, nor could they goad her into using soap or a comb. She was a whittled widow, eroded to the lowest of the low—a place where only those who have lost their closest friend could really know.

About the Author

Though *Trapped in the Cracks* is my first complete work of fiction, I have been an ardent writer of prose and poetry for many years, and an avid reader, of everything from comics to classics, most of my life.

Like a weary horse to water, in times of despair, I have always found my way back to the banks of a clear flowing stream of weaved words. As a young kid attempting to grow, seemingly in the midst of a storm, I sought distraction from the disheartening circumstances in which I was born. To maintain calm within as my world was whipped with wind, I wrote. I jotted drafts of short stories and filled callouts with the dialogue of my imagined and illustrated characters in my own amateur comic books. As a child, outside of completing one of my many absorbing drawings of clawed or caped villains and heroes, I rarely found a sincere reason to smile.

My adoration of beautifully crafted prose and poetry prompted me to sculpt my own inspiring works of art from the expressive clay of boundless words. When I unexpectedly won an essay contest as a sophomore, my potential for writing was realized. However, seldom truly restful, my youth was stressful. And, as a young adult, hastily penned poems became the therapeutic medicine that kept depression and stress at bay, as I repeated the lie that everything would be okay.

Though it is purely fiction pulled from my imagination, *Trapped in the Cracks* was greatly influenced by the experiences of friends, family members, neighbors, and myself, while growing up in Gary, Indiana in the '90s. This was a particularly dismal decade for the city. Through distribution, addiction or imprisonment, nearly every family was touched by crack cocaine or heroin. Some were rocked in all three ways, by both drugs. Ensuing gang struggles over territory and profit skyrocketed Gary's per capita murder rate—at times exceeding that of major U.S. cities. My most enduring memories of this bleak period are of nights when the sheer volume of gunfire was mind-bogglingly senseless; and seeing addicts—who to me, at a young age, looked like metamorphosing zombies—seemingly strewn like litter up and down stairwells, spilling in and out of homes and aimlessly drifting down dreary streets.

Besides spending much of my youth in the ghettos of Gary, other life experiences that influenced this work include three proud years of service in the U.S. Army; nearly two years of justly warranted, but definitely not regretted (For the many lessons the isolation and quiet allowed me to evaluate and learn about myself, life, and the world, at a time when, unbeknownst to me at twenty years of age, I actually understood so little.), incarceration; and nearly eighteen total months living in NYC homeless shelters. Through it all, I read.

Authors who have had a profound influence on me over the years include James Baldwin, Miguel de Cervantes, Ralph Ellison, Toni Morrison, George Orwell, James Patterson, Edgar Allan Poe, and Charles Saunders. Some of my favorite books of fiction are *Don Quixote, The Pillars of the Earth, Invisible Man, Beloved, Home, Tar Baby, Sula, Animal Farm, 1984, Imaro,*

Kiss the Girls, Memoirs of a Geisha, The Coldest Winter Ever, The Alchemist, Angles and Demons, The Count of Monte Cristo, The Stand, Giovanni's Room and *Crime and Punishment*, amongst many others.

My obsession with intricate rhyme schemes and alliteration came from reading the poetry of Edgar Allan Poe and General George S. Patton and listening on repeat to the verses of 2pac, AZ, Big Daddy Kane, Big L, Big Pun, Canibus, Common, Dead Prez, DMX, Eminem, Immortal Technique, Jadakiss, Kool G Rap, Nas, Papoose, Rakim, Scarface, The Notorious B.I.G., T.I. and Young Jeezy.

I was born and raised in Gary, Indiana. After seven years in the borough of Brooklyn, I relocated to Milwaukee, Wisconsin, where I currently reside.

"There have been times when law enforcement officers, because of the laws enacted by federal, state and local governments, have been the face of oppression to far too many of our fellow citizens. In the past, the laws adopted by our society have required police officers to perform many unpalatable tasks, such as ensuring legalized discrimination or even denying the basic rights of citizenship to many of our fellow Americans. While this is no longer the case, this dark side of our shared history has created a multigenerational—almost inherited—mistrust between many communities of color and their law enforcement agencies."

-Chief Terrence M. Cunningham, former President, and current Deputy Executive Director of the International Association of Chiefs of Police, issuing a formal apology on the group's behalf for historical mistreatment of communities of color

"But if you dismiss black complaints of mistreatment by police as being completely rooted in our modern context, then you're missing the point completely. There has never been a period in our history where the law and order branch of the state has not operated against the freedoms, the liberties, the options, the choices that have been available to the black community, generally speaking. And to ignore that racial heritage, to ignore that historical context, means you can't have an informed debate about the current state of blacks and police relationship today, 'cause this didn't just appear out of nothing. This is the product of a centuries-long historical process. And to not reckon with that is to shut off solutions."

-Dr. Kevin Gannon,
Professor of History, and Director of the Center for Excellence in Teaching and Learning (CETL), at Grand View University

"We knew we couldn't make it illegal to be either against the war or black. But by getting the public to associate the hippies with marijuana and blacks with heroin and then criminalizing both heavily, we could disrupt their communities. We could arrest their leaders, raid their homes, break up their meetings, and vilify them night after night on the evening news. Did we know we were lying about the drugs? Of course, we did."

- John Ehrlichman,
Chief Domestic Advisor for President Richard Nixon

"…when it came to public policy, my response was "lock them up," instead of the more compassionate—and let's face it, difficult—response of "let's get them treatment." So what I am struck by now is how my perspective has changed. Sure, I'm a few decades older and have learned some things, but it's worth noting what crack meant to us. It meant *black street crime*. Today, what the opioid epidemic means for many of us: *Whites need treatment*."

- Ed Stetzer,
Executive Director of the Billy Graham Center at Wheaton College, in an article about double standards in responding to the crack crisis vs. the opioid epidemic

"The opioid epidemic has, at least recently, been met with empathy, creativity, and heart. The crack epidemic of the 1980s was met with scorn and punishment. The rhetoric around crack painted addicts as wild animals, "super-predators" who needed to be brought to "heel." It was easier for lawmakers, pundits and the like to separate themselves from the crisis, as nearly all of them were white and well-off. The crack epidemic almost exclusively impacted people of color living in poor neighborhoods—it was a problem of another world. This made it far easier to implement draconian policies that actively dehumanized those afflicted."

-Jesse Mechanic,
Editor in Chief at The Overgrown, Politics Blogger at The Huff Post, Clinic Researcher at Beth Israel

"We can have democracy in this country, or we can have great wealth concentrated in the hands of a few, but we can't have both."

-Lewis Brandeis,
Associate Justice of the Supreme Court of the United States (in office 1916-1939)